Stefanie gazed at him. "Do you still think that the two deaths are connected in some way?"

Campbell sat back contemplatively, then replied with a catch to his voice, "My gut instinct says yes. But the facts, as they are currently, may tell a different story. I suppose I'll just have to keep digging till the right answers surface one way or another. In the meantime, I have someone else who's occupying my attention these days..."

Feeling the weight of his steady gaze, Stefanie couldn't help but color as she asked playfully, "And who might that be?"

"You, Stefanie," he said clearly and concisely.

Her cheeks reddened with satisfaction. "You're occupying my attention just as much these days, Campbell," she stated candidly.

He grinned. "Good to know."

CARNIVAL COLD CASE

R. BARRI FLOWERS

INTRIGUE

If you purchased this book without a cover you should be aware that this book is stolen property. It was reported as "unsold and destroyed" to the publisher, and neither the author nor the publisher has received any payment for this "stripped book."

In fond memory of my beloved mother, Marjah Aljean, a devoted lifelong fan of Harlequin romance and romantic suspense novels, who inspired me to excel in my personal and professional lives. To H. Loraine (a mermaid at heart), the true and dearest love of my life and very best friend, whose support has been unwavering through the many terrific years together. To the many loyal and lasting fans of my romance, suspense, mystery, thriller and young adult fiction published over the years. A special shout-out goes to a wonderful group of talents whom I have long admired: Carol, Charmian, Hedy, Krista, Lisa, Peggy, Olivia and Sharon. And last but not least, a nod to my superb Harlequin editors, Emma Cole and Susan Litman, for the wonderful opportunity to lend my literary voice and creative spirit to the enormously successful Intrigue line, as well as Miranda Indrigo, the wonderful concierge, who serendipitously led me to great success with Harlequin Intrigue.

ISBN-13: 978-1-335-69059-3

Recycling programs for this product may not exist in your area.

Carnival Cold Case

Copyright © 2026 by R. Barri Flowers

All rights reserved. No part of this book may be used or reproduced in any manner whatsoever without written permission.

Without limiting the exclusive rights of any author, contributor or the publisher of this publication, any unauthorized use of this publication to train generative artificial intelligence (AI) technologies is expressly prohibited. Harlequin also exercises their rights under Article 4(3) of the Digital Single Market Directive 2019/790 and expressly reserves this publication from the text and data mining exception.

This is a work of fiction. Names, characters, places and incidents are either the product of the author's imagination or are used fictitiously. Any resemblance to actual persons, living or dead, businesses, companies, events or locales is entirely coincidental.

For questions and comments about the quality of this book, please contact us at CustomerService@Harlequin.com.

TM and ® are trademarks of Harlequin Enterprises ULC.

Harlequin Enterprises ULC
22 Adelaide St. West, 41st Floor
Toronto, Ontario M5H 4E3, Canada
www.Harlequin.com

HarperCollins Publishers
Macken House, 39/40 Mayor Street Upper,
Dublin 1, D01 C9W8, Ireland
www.HarperCollins.com

Printed in Lithuania

R. Barri Flowers is an award-winning author of crime, thriller, mystery and romance fiction featuring three-dimensional protagonists, riveting plots, unexpected twists and turns, and heart-pounding climaxes. With an expertise in true crime, serial killers and characterizing dangerous offenders, he is perfectly suited for the Harlequin Intrigue line. Chemistry and conflict between the hero and heroine, attention to detail and incorporating the very latest advances in criminal investigations are the cornerstones of his romantic suspense fiction. Discover more on popular social networks and Wikipedia.

Books by R. Barri Flowers

Harlequin Intrigue

Criminal Case Files

Explosion at the Marina
Carnival Cold Case

Bureaus of Investigation Mysteries

Killer in Shellview County
Hiding in Alaska
Christmas Bank Heists
Hunting a Predator

The Lynleys of Law Enforcement

Special Agent Witness
Christmas Lights Killer
Murder in the Blue Ridge Mountains
Cold Murder in Kolton Lake
Campus Killer
Mississippi Manhunt

Visit the Author Profile page at Harlequin.com.

CAST OF CHARACTERS

Stefanie Nguyen—A widow and yoga and tai chi instructor. She stumbles upon a body on Founders' Day in Reston Hills, Idaho, her new home, and works with a handsome police detective to solve a widening mystery, as sparks fly between them.

Campbell Sawyer—A detective with the Reston Hills Police Department who investigates a drug-overdose death that is eerily reminiscent of a similar unsolved homicide twenty years earlier. Are the cases related? Should he be worried for the safety of the attractive widow who's caught his eye?

Mason Sawyer—A retired police detective and widower who is still haunted by the one case he couldn't crack. Will he get a second chance, with the help of his son, to finally get much-needed answers?

Georgina Alvarez—A dedicated police detective who is determined to help solve two drug-induced homicides that hit too close to home.

Bella Reston—A local historian whose great-grandfather Arthur Reston founded the town. What lengths will she go to to protect her family's legacy?

Kenneth Braison—The leader of the Braison Family, following in his father's footsteps. Both are suspects in deaths of cult members by poisoning. But could looks be deceiving? Or deadly accurate?

Prologue

Lynda Boxleitner felt tense as she walked down the sidewalk shortly after midnight. She was scheduled to work at a food truck in a few hours, dishing out corn dogs, tacos and more food items to anyone who wanted them during the Founder's Day festivities that were held each year like clockwork in Reston Hills, Idaho. But before that, she had volunteered to ride in the parade. She was a former high school cheerleader, still shapely and nice on the eyes—if she thought so herself—even at forty-one and three months, to be exact.

Unfortunately, that had proved to be as much a liability as an asset, given the precarious predicament she now found herself in, much as she hated to admit it.

Lynda moved briskly across the concrete, which was damp from the drizzle that was coming down steadily as if it had nothing better to do, matting her long and curly blond hair. She needed to get home, assess the situation and then hope she hadn't gotten in over her head in the worst possible way.

Or had she played her hand just right—much like her late father, Garrison Boxleitner, a former card shark who plied his trade on riverboat casinos once upon a time? She believed she was entitled to be happy just like everyone else. She was an independent woman who had come too far in life to be simply dismissed as an unworthy piece of trash.

She needed to stand up for herself. Certainly no one else was going to. Least of all the powerful man whom Lynda had given everything to, only to receive far too little in return, just empty promises and veiled threats. Or did they go further than that?

Now it was time to turn the tables. But was she being smart about it? Or had she gone too far in making demands that, even to herself, she was beginning to have second thoughts about?

Lynda's reverie was interrupted as she heard footsteps from behind, causing her bold blue eyes to have a quick look over her shoulder. She didn't see anyone. Had she imagined it? Maybe so. And yet her instincts told her someone was watching. Waiting. A real threat.

I have to get out of this rain and inside my apartment, where I'll be safe, she told herself, picking up the pace despite wearing slingback pumps that were uncomfortable on her feet. Her wrap cocktail dress was getting soaked.

It was only in that moment that she began to feel queasy, seemingly coming out of nowhere. This was followed by severe abdominal pains, causing her to flinch from the discomfort. Suddenly, she began to retch the cheeseburger and ranch fries she'd had for dinner.

What's happening to me? Lynda asked herself, frantic, as she tried to remain upright and make it back to her apartment. Someway. Somehow. She thought she heard more footsteps and turned around, but again saw no one. Was she hallucinating? Or flat-out losing her mind?

Something was terribly wrong with her. But what? And why?

Her coordination became impaired as she had trouble maintaining her balance. Blurriness set in like a thick fog for everything around her, and it became hard to breathe.

Just as she was beginning to figure out what was possibly behind her condition, Lynda felt her legs give out from beneath her as if slipping on ice. She fell flat on her face, breaking her nose in the process. But by that time, she had already become numb to her painful ordeal, losing consciousness before ever realizing she had breathed her last breath as the rain fell cruelly upon her lifeless body.

THE DARK SUV had slowly but surely trailed her, making sure to keep its distance. Till she dropped like a sack of potatoes and there was no escaping her fate.

He pulled up alongside the fallen woman, who had given him far more trouble than he wanted. And now she was paying the ultimate price for getting out of line, threatening to disrupt, in a major and unacceptable way, all that he stood for.

Getting out of the vehicle under the cover of darkness, he approached her and checked for a pulse. Happy to see there wasn't even the slightest hint of one, he lifted her up, ignoring the blood that oozed from her broken nose and onto the sleeve of his bomber jacket. He swiftly loaded her into the back of the SUV.

After climbing into the driver's seat, he drove off and soon turned onto a side road in a wooded area. Away from any possible prying eyes, he removed her clothing and shoes while thinking about how much he'd loved seeing her shapely stark-naked body when things were good between them.

Almost too good, in fact.

But that was then. And this was now.

She had gotten way two big for her britches. It left him no other choice than to remind her of just who was calling the shots in this little arrangement between them.

It sure as hell wasn't you, he cursed to himself with a combination of satisfaction and relief. And she had no one else to blame for having her life snuffed out like a candle.

Driving again, he got back on the main road, which soon turned into Hepmore Avenue, where the Founder's Day parade would commence in a few hours, en route to Reston Hills Park.

Getting there ahead of time, knowing he would be participating in the revelries just like damn near everyone in town, he parked but left the engine running.

After dragging the corpse out of the back of the SUV, he deliberately left her in a spot where she couldn't be missed. The sooner her death became public knowledge, the sooner it could lead to an investigation that would have the intended results.

Though, if he were honest with himself, there would be mild regrets and lingering fantasies of what might have been. But he fully intended to get on with his life as though she had never entered and upended it in the first place.

After all, what other choice did he have?

He got back inside the SUV and drove off, content he'd rid himself of a problem that had to be solved without boomeranging back at him in the worst possible way.

Reston Hills Police Department Detective Mason Sawyer had planned to take off for the better part of Founder's Day and enjoy the yearly celebration with his gorgeous wife, Alyssa, and teenage son, Campbell, knowing just how important quality family time was. Especially in his line of work, when career obligations and professional aspirations tended to win out over a personal life.

But that wasn't happening. At least not yet.

As was often the case at inopportune times, duty called, and he had no other choice but to answer.

A report came in of a naked dead woman found in Reston Hills Park by workers this morning as they were setting up the stage for a concert.

With half the staff off and without needing to be asked by his boss, Lieutenant Gloria Schecter, Mason volunteered to scrub his off day—or at least delay it till further notice—and check it out. As he had serious designs to move up to her position someday, it was always important to show his dependability when others chose to put their own needs first.

As he drove his unmarked vehicle down Hepmore Avenue, Mason knew his wife, loving as she was, would understand. Hadn't that always been true, ever since she chose to take the plunge and marry a dedicated police officer twenty years ago, when they were both in their early twenties? This didn't make him feel any better. He would make it up to her by taking her out to dinner at her favorite restaurant in town. But his son was a different story altogether. Campbell needed that quality dad time to stay engaged, maintain discipline, and keep himself on the straight and narrow path in his life.

I'll make it up to you, too, Campbell, if this turns out to be something other than an accidental death, Mason reflected, scratching into his short black flat-top hair, then smoothing his pyramid mustache. His first thought was that the woman's death could be drug related, knowing that they had a drug problem in Reston Hills, like most big and small towns in the United States. Sadly, overdoses were not uncommon there.

Homicides were, relatively speaking. But he wouldn't jump to conclusions just yet.

Somehow it felt a bit unseemly to kill someone on Founder's Day. As if a killer would take that into consideration prior to ending a person's life.

After he arrived at the park and conferred with the first responder, Jerry Napolitano—an officer around his age and six foot two in height, with brown hair in a buzz cut—they made their way through tall Norway maple and Douglas fir trees to the scene.

Mason took one look at the deceased fortysomething woman and his jaw dropped. Lying awkwardly on her back, her pale white body was exposed for all to see. Blue eyes were open vacantly, her small nose was clearly fractured and discolored, and her full mouth slightly parted as though in total shock that this had happened to her. The long blond hair splayed around her head haphazardly was damp, suggesting she had been there when it was still raining till at least the wee hours of the morning. He noted the reddish-purple marking on her right forearm, which resembled initials.

Mason gulped. He knew her.

Lynda Boxleitner.

They had dated briefly in high school, but she was,

quite frankly, more than he could handle at the time, as an attractive cheerleader who had her pick of suitors. It became apparent to him that he was not what she was looking for in a boyfriend for the long term, and both moved in different directions. He'd only spoken to her casually from time to time since then.

Now she was dead.

Mason had a gut feeling that it wasn't a suicide. She didn't seem the type to go there, from what he knew of her. And judging by the positioning of the body, it certainly didn't seem like an accident.

Whether drugs had played a part in Lynda's untimely death remained to be seen.

As did the precise nature of death, which, at the moment, he had to believe was a probable homicide, making the ghastly scenario that much harder to swallow.

Chapter One

Twenty years later

She felt cold, clammy, maybe a little weird and definitely disoriented. But not so out of it so as to not realize she was totally naked.

She couldn't exactly remember removing the knit off-the-shoulder top, ripped straight-leg jeans and flats she'd been wearing.

Yet here she was, and in the park, way past midnight but well before dawn—running almost blindly through the tall, thick trees.

And she wasn't alone.

Someone was chasing her. Someone she knew all too well. And another person, not so much.

They wanted to kill her. To silence her forever.

She wanted to live. But could she realistically outrun them? When they were as determined to catch up to her as she was to evade them with every fiber inside her?

She sucked in a deep, ragged breath—her breathing more and more laborious. Her heart was racing, too, as if wanting to burst through her chest.

What was wrong with her?

What had they to done to her?

She bit back the pain from the blisters on the bottom of her feet from the pounding they took while running across hard dirt and rocks, but she didn't dare slow down.

If only she could get through the trail and find a place to hide from them. Till someone could help her.

Or was it already too late for that, her fate sealed?

As dizziness and queasiness seemed to hit her all at once like a ton of bricks, her thin legs started to give out.

The last thing she remembered before the lights went out for good was that she had gone about things the wrong way. Underestimating her adversary in the process.

And she would never have the chance to rethink her bad choices.

THE FOUNDER'S DAY CELEBRATION, on a Sunday in late June, was in full swing with a colorful parade featuring floats, riders, marching bands, walkers and cheering onlookers as it moved slowly down Hepmore Avenue toward Reston Hills Park, where there were carnival rides—including a Ferris wheel, jumbo slide and a carousel for kids—inflatables, arts and crafts, face painting, entertainers, and business and food vendors eager to market their goods and outdo one another.

Stefanie Nguyen was excited to attend her first Founder's Day event since moving to Reston Hills, Idaho, four months ago from San Antonio, Texas. A Vietnamese American widow at thirty-four, after losing her firefighter husband, Edward Nguyen, two years earlier in the line of duty, Stefanie had made the painful decision to sell their Spanish Colonial home for a fresh start. She was sure Edward would have applauded her decision, not wanting her to dwell on the tragic ending of their marriage and get on with her life as best as possible. To that end, she'd reluctantly removed the wedding ring from her finger, knowing it was time to let go of the past and have a clean slate as a single woman.

Stefanie believed her late parents, John and Brenda Linh, would also have approved of a fresh start for her, having always instilled in her a sense of looking forward rather than backward in terms of making choices that put her needs first and foremost. She'd chosen Reston Hills for its small-town hospitality and traditional values, much like the place where she grew up in Limestone County, Texas. Though her late husband's life insurance, investments and personal savings had provided her the financial means to live anywhere comfortably, Stefanie preferred to work at least part-time, as she had previously. Putting to good use her master's degree in Exercise Physiology from the University of Texas at Austin's Department of Kinesiology and Health Education, she taught yoga three times a week and tai chi twice a week in her new setting, and liked to jog and swim as part of her personal fitness routine.

At the moment, she was enjoying the Founder's Day festivities at the park—which, beyond that, for her, often included hiking on nature trails near and along the banks of the Beeks River. Running a hand through long and straight black hair that fell across her shoulders, Stefanie's small brown eyes regarded the local musicians on the main stage. They were performing everything from country to easy listening to blues to jazz music—much to the delight of those who had gathered around, judging by the foot stomping and hips swaying left and right joyously.

Though she was beginning to feel right at home and

had made a few friends since moving there, Stefanie still found herself lonely at times. There had been no one romantically in her life since Edward, save for a date or two that went nowhere. She longed for a day when that might change but wouldn't rush it. When the time was right, she was sure someone suitable would come along.

"Hey, you," Stefanie heard a soft voice say over her shoulder.

She moved her slip-on white sneakers around and looked into the bold green eyes of Bella Reston, whose great-grandfather Arthur Reston was the namesake of the town. Bella, the Founder's Day committee chair, who also ran a private foundation for charitable causes, was the same age as Stefanie, just as slender and about an inch taller. A divorcée—or happily single, as Bella liked to put it—she was gorgeous by any stretch of the imagination, with golden blond hair in a blunt mid-length cut. The two had hit it off after Bella took one of her yoga classes a couple of months ago and later talked her into volunteering to help promote the event and recruit other volunteers to do whatever was necessary to make it a big success.

Stefanie, who was wearing a multicolored split-neck sleeveless blouse and beige twill pants, put a smile on her face. "Hey."

Bella had on a green halter midi dress, which flattered her figure, and wedge sandals. She smiled back and, gazing at the stage, asked, "So, are they any good?"

"They're terrific," Stefanie had to say truthfully. "Definitely keeping everyone engaged."

"Glad to hear it." Bella lifted her dimpled chin. "Let's just hope I can do the same."

Stefanie knew that as the chairperson—with the appropriate genealogy—Bella would be taking the stage momentarily to sing the praises of Reston Hills and its journey to becoming a thriving town in Idaho. "You'll have them eating out of your hands."

Bella laughed. "I don't know if I'd go that far, but it's very sweet of you to say anyway."

Stefanie touched Bella's arm and said, "Hey, it's in your blood. And it's not like you haven't been down this road before." As she understood it, Bella had chaired the committee for the past three years and, given that she'd continued to hold the position, was obviously good at what she did.

"True." Bella took a breath and slipped an errant strand of hair behind her ear. "Well, wish me luck anyhow."

"Good luck," Stefanie told her and laughed. "Not that you'll need it."

"Thanks." She flashed her white teeth. "Hope not."

As Bella made her way to the stage, Stefanie checked her cell phone for messages. There were no new ones. Just as she was slipping the phone back into her pocket, a slender twentysomething African American woman with a blond Afro-puff hairstyle approached her and said in an affable tone, "Hi."

"Hi," Stefanie returned.

"My name's Jasmine," she said, gazing at her with big brown eyes. "I was wondering if you've heard about the Braison Family?"

Stefanie cocked a thin brow. "Actually, I haven't."

"They're a great group of people who love each other, love freedom, love nature and a whole lot more."

"Hmm… Sounds interesting," Stefanie said, for lack of a better response.

"It really is," Jasmine gushed. She pulled out a flyer from her shoulder tote. "You should check it out yourself. We have get-togethers regularly. I promise you won't be disappointed."

Stefanie took the flyer out of courtesy but didn't imagine it was something she would pursue. Even if she had no problem with camaraderie among like-minded individuals, per se. She had enough on her plate for the time being. "Maybe I will give it a try," she told her nonetheless.

"Cool." Jasmine gave her a toothy smile. "What's your name?"

"Stefanie."

"Well, Stefanie, hope to see you there." She walked away, only to approach someone else with the same obviously rehearsed but convincing lines.

Stefanie watched briefly in amusement as she stuck the flyer in the pocket of her pants, not wanting to litter. She would dispose of it later.

Turning her attention to the stage, Stefanie regarded Bella, who was in the process of charming her audience in a cool-headed, relatable way by masterfully bridging the past to the present on Founder's Day.

"My great-grandfather Arthur Reston had a vision when he founded the town that bears his name, Reston Hills, more than a century ago," Bella was saying. "He wanted this to be a place where hardworking, family-loving, God-fearing Americans could make a good life for themselves—make that *great*—symbolizing the spirit of community that we've all come to love and cherish. My grandfather Malcolm Reston dutifully followed in his mighty footsteps, in promoting the town and its core values. My late father, Stuart Reston, stepped into their shoes with the same dedication. And now it's my turn to make them all proud—and you, too. Let's make sure that the rich tradition we all embody in Reston Hills shall live on as we celebrate another marvelous Founder's Day—"

Stefanie grinned at a job well done by her friend as Bella received applause before leaving the stage and circulating among the townsfolk dutifully while the musicians returned.

I think this is a good time for some me time, Stefanie told herself as she meandered her way through the crowd, seemingly unnoticed by most, who were too caught up in themselves or each other. She headed toward a part of the park near the river that was less likely to be too occupied while the festivities were underway. She had no problem with any mild-mannered wildlife she might encounter. *I won't complain if some western meadowlarks want to sing to me*, she thought wittily.

Just as she started to head down a trail, Stefanie was stopped cold as she came upon a naked body. It was that of a young and slender white female with dark, short hair and small breasts. She was lying flat on her back atop some undergrowth. What looked to be initials were noticeably tattooed on her pale right forearm, as if to make a statement.

Sucking in a deep breath, Stefanie could only imagine how the pretty twentysomething woman had ended up there without any clothes on. But she didn't need much imagination to believe that she was looking at the pallid face of a corpse.

RESTON HILLS POLICE DEPARTMENT Detective Campbell Sawyer sat at the counter of Harriette's Café on Pickford

Street, named for its longtime owner Harriette Yardley, musingly sipping coffee with a dash of cream. He probably should have been at the Founder's Day celebration like a number of his coworkers—some on duty, others off—but he figured they could survive without him. Not that he hadn't attended enough of them since he was five years old—probably too many to count.

But it was different now. Or seemed that way. He simply couldn't muster up the same enthusiasm from years past to be an active participant. Even if he was proud to be a member of the community, which was thriving insofar as relatively small towns could thrive. Reston Hills was in Eckerslin County—one hundred and seventy-five miles from Boise, but it might as well be a thousand miles away with regard to its down-to-earth, laidback lifestyle where people largely stayed out of other people's business unless invited in.

He should know. Prior to the last three and a half years, he had lived in Boise, where Campbell worked for the Boise Police Department as a detective in the Criminal Investigation Division's Violent Crimes Unit, Narcotics Unit and Crimes Against Children division at varying times during his ten-plus years with the force. Prior to that, he had attended Boise State University, where he'd received a Bachelor of Science degree in Criminal Justice.

But burnout and a high-stress environment, along with a longing to reestablish roots in his hometown, brought him back to Reston Hills. The fact that there was an opening at the detective level with the Reston Hills PD's Investigation Division, for which he came highly recommended by his former boss, Captain Mick Fernandez, made it a done deal.

Campbell hadn't looked back, having settled into life again in Reston Hills—now at age thirty-six, with few complaints to speak of. He had reconnected with his father, Mason Sawyer, a retired police detective who had a horse ranch not far from town. Though they hadn't always seen eye to eye, the real love and respect had been there throughout. Especially after Campbell had lost his mother, Alyssa Sawyer, a decade ago to breast cancer. He and his father had taken it hard, neither seeming to find the right words to say to each other in dealing with the death. But they had slowly worked their way through and come to terms with it.

Campbell ran a hand through his black hair, which was cut short but was long enough to appreciate. He put the coffee mug to his lips, just below a Dallas mustache. About the only thing missing at the moment in his life was romance. Or something resembling an intimate relationship. Since breaking up with his last girlfriend, Naomi Espelita, while still living in Boise, he'd remained frustratingly single, with only an occasional date here and there to fill the void of loneliness unsuccessfully.

Oh well, I'll just have to wait it out till the right woman comes along and let the chips fall where they may—hoping they fall in the right direction, toward a real future together, Campbell thought, finishing up the coffee.

No sooner had he set the empty cup on the counter when the waitress was before him almost on cue with the pot of coffee in her hand.

"Care for a refill?" she asked, a flirtatious smile playing on her full lips.

Campbell cast his blue eyes at Sarah Huffstetler, in her late twenties and voluptuous inside the tight taupe uniform. She had thick blond hair with parted bangs. They had gone out on exactly one date, which was all it took for him to realize they weren't meant for each other. Though he had expressed this in the nicest way possible, he suspected she may have felt otherwise and had apparently not gotten the message.

He gave a sideways grin and, lifting a hand as if to ward off a blow, responded, "Thanks, Sarah, but I'm good."

She looked disappointed but seemed to recover quickly. "Had to ask."

"I know, and I appreciate the service." Campbell stood to his full height of six feet, two and three-quarter inches, towering over her at just over five feet tall. "See you next time around."

Sarah licked her lips invitingly. "I'll be here."

That's what I'm afraid of, he thought sardonically, but actually had no problem with them being on friendly terms, even a little flirtatious from her end. So long as it went no further than that.

After stepping outside into the fresh—albeit a bit humid—air and bright sunshine, while feeling this was perfect weather for the Founder's Day events, Campbell's cell phone rang. He removed it from the back pocket of his tweed pants and answered in his strong detective's voice, "Yeah?"

"We got a report of a dead naked female in Reston Hills Park," the dispatcher said tonelessly, as if it was no big deal.

Campbell frowned, believing otherwise, as every life was precious to him. Without considering the circumstances of the deceased, he hated the thought that anyone—on this, of all days—should have to die and be deprived of a future and all the positive things it could entail. "I'm on my way," he muttered, walking toward the parking lot.

He climbed into his cypress-gray Chevy Tahoe SUV and headed for the park while wondering if the victim had succumbed to a drug overdose. Or other means of avoidable death. Those were always the worst circumstances, when someone's life was cut short through no fault of their own.

Arriving at his destination, Campbell took a routine peek at the Glock 19 Gen5 9x19mm duty pistol that was concealed in a paddle holster inside his wool blazer. He turned his attention to the festival, which was still in full swing—a good sign, since the community depended on the revenue earned by businesses that used Founder's Day to generate year-round exposure. Not to mention, the last thing anyone needed was to take away from the spirit of the important day in the town's history through tragedy.

Once the cause of death was determined, a period of adjustment could be made accordingly.

Campbell flashed his identification to Officer Eli Gundersen, a twenty-five-year-old rookie who was tall and muscular with red hair in a crew cut.

"We've got a strange one here..." Eli said, a catch to his voice as he rubbed his jawline.

"I can see that." Campbell was inclined to agree as he took a look at the deceased white female laying awkwardly on her back in the nude at the spot, with other officers keeping the public at bay. He guessed her to be in her mid-twenties. She had jet-black hair in a bob style and was maybe five-five or so. There were cuts on her arms, legs and feet that may have come from being in the park naked. But no outward signs of foul play or otherwise significant distress of the corpse.

He zoomed in on her thin forearm and noticed the initials that appeared to be "KB" tattooed on it. That rang an immediate bell with him. Members of a local cult calling itself the Braison Family were being branded with the initials of its controversial leader, Kenneth Braison. Campbell had visited their compound before, investigating reported drug activity that had proved inconclusive. Was she—or had she been—a member of the cult?

"What are your thoughts?" Eli asked curiously.

Campbell couldn't help but think back to a similar case his father had encountered as a police detective twenty years ago that involved a fatally poisoned woman, in what turned out to be a homicide that eventually became a cold case. It had dogged his father for the rest of his career and had never been solved to this day, as far as Campbell was aware. "Well, I'm still working on that," he responded contemplatively. "Any sign of her clothing…or a cell phone…?"

"Not yet." Eli looked off into the distance. "She either ended up here without them, or someone took them after she died."

Campbell pondered this. "Do you know who she is?" Though most people seemed to know one another in a small town, to one degree or another, this wasn't always the case. Especially for those affiliated with the Braison Family, who tended to maintain a low profile in a concerted effort at staying under the radar from law enforcement. Not to mention, the Founder's Day celebration typically attracted visitors from elsewhere.

"Haven't seen her before," Eli answered succinctly. "At least, not that I can recall."

Campbell took that as a no. Or maybe as a newly married man, the officer felt uncomfortable in saying otherwise, as if it made him look guilty of her death just by association. Campbell chose to give him the benefit of the doubt, considering Eli had given himself some wiggle room by not insisting that he hadn't seen her before in any way, shape or form.

Focusing his gaze again on the dead woman, Campbell felt a touch of familiarity, as if they had crossed paths before, in one way or another. He strained his eyes for recognition. He was usually pretty good at pinning to memory those he'd crossed paths with, even if with little more than a passing glance. But in this instance, he came up empty. Maybe this was the very first time he'd seen her face—and body. And, if so, it would certainly be memorable moving forward.

Campbell turned back to Eli and asked, "Who discovered the body?"

Before the officer could respond, Campbell heard a female's voice say in an elevated tone, "I did."

He gazed out beyond the yellow crime scene tape's established perimeter and laid eyes on a gorgeous and slender Asian woman in her early thirties, with long dark hair. Walking over to her, he got past his initial reaction to her as someone who was totally his type—to the degree that he had any real type, as such—and said professionally, "Hi. I'm Detective Campbell Sawyer."

"Stefanie Nguyen."

Campbell took a moment to gaze into the arresting brown eyes on her heart-shaped face, with a thin nose that was slightly upturned, and a small mouth. He then said evenly, "Ms. Nguyen, can you tell me how you came upon the deceased, if you saw anyone else near the body—and anything more you care to say about this…?"

Stefanie swallowed and replied, with a catch to her voice, "I can try my best."

For the time being, that was about all Campbell could ask for from her. Beyond that, he was more than willing to keep an open mind.

Chapter Two

Stefanie was still trying to come to terms with finding a dead body along the trail. It was quite literally the last thing she'd expected to see when stepping away from the music and other Founder's Day events for a bit of solitude. But here she was, face-to-face with an extremely handsome detective named Campbell Sawyer—albeit on opposite sides of the crime scene tape—who was investigating the mysterious death. She loved his Dallas mustache, which was a perfect fit for his square-jawed features, Greek nose and penetrating blue eyes, as well as the coal-colored hair in a short quiff. He was wearing a dark blue blazer over a light blue checkered button-down shirt and gray tweed pants, along with black monk-strap shoes.

Once she caught her breath, Stefanie met his gaze and said, in a measured tone of voice, "I'd just left the area where music was playing, to be by myself, and was planning to walk down the trail and along the river...when I saw her—" Stefanie glanced in the direction of the body, trying not to freak out. She looked back at the detective. "I never saw anyone near her—only people that were hanging out along the way, seemingly oblivious to what had happened to the poor woman—"

Campbell nodded. "Did you happen to recognize her?"

"No." Stefanie flinched. "I'm not from around here—just moved to Reston Hills four months ago—so I haven't had much of an opportunity to familiarize myself with too many faces as of yet." *TMI*, she thought, but still felt compelled to put it out there.

"I see." He pinched an aquiline nose. "Where are you from?"

"San Antonio."

"Texas?" he said thoughtfully. "Nice state."

"It is," she agreed, missing the state more than she cared to admit but content in knowing the time was right to relocate. She returned to the moment at hand. "I wish I had gotten to know her—the dead woman—and maybe… I don't know, through one means or another, have been able to somehow help her avoid her fate—" *He probably thinks I'm just babbling just for the sake of it and maybe I am*, she told herself, still a little nervous about the situation.

"That would have been great," he said in a gentle voice. "But unfortunately, these things happen—sad as that is—even though none of us ever want it to. Or can control it."

"You're right." Stefanie wrung her hands. "Doesn't make it go down any easier."

"For you and me both," Campbell assured her. "Know that I'll do everything I can to find out who she is and how she ended up dead in the park."

His hard expression told her he meant business. This was comforting to Stefanie, as she felt very much that no one deserved to be humiliated in death. Even if it came by one's own hand, there would certainly have been a trigger to bring her to that point. And if there were nefarious reasons the life was taken away, there was further cause to get to the bottom of it and get justice for the victim.

"I'm sure you're good at your job, Detective," Stefanie told him instinctively. She looked over his shoulder at the deceased woman and the personnel from the Eckerslin County Coroner's Office, who would remove the body. Gazing back at him, she said evenly, "I just hope she can be at peace when you have your answers."

"Me, too." Campbell reached into his pants pocket and removed a card. "We may need you to come in and give a formal statement. Other than that, if anything pops into your head—big or small—relating to this investigation, call me anytime on either number there..." He handed her the card.

Stefanie took a quick look at the info and nodded. "Will do," she promised.

"Then I'll let you get back to your Founder's Day activities."

She furrowed her brow. "Not sure I'm quite up to that," she admitted, hardly in the mood for fun and frolic after what she'd seen. Instead, she intended to go home. "But thanks anyway."

Campbell flashed her an understanding look and said smoothly, as if he could predict the future, "See you later."

Stefanie couldn't help but feel enthusiastic about the prospect of seeing him again as she watched the detective walk back toward the others on that side of the barrier.

She turned in the opposite direction, in search of Bella, to share the sad news with her. *I almost hate to rain on her parade*, Stefanie told herself, knowing how much Founder's Day meant to Bella as part of her family's legacy. But she would learn about the tragedy sooner or later—

as would everyone who lived in Reston Hills—so there was no need to withhold it from her.

STEFANIE PULLED BELLA away from an elderly member of the Founder's Day committee, wanting to be the first to bring her up to speed on the grim discovery as the one true friend she had in town.

"There you are," Bella told her spiritedly. "I was looking for you to see what you thought of my speech—if you could call it that."

"It was wonderful," Stefanie said sincerely. "You would've made your grandfather and father proud." Bella had lost her dad, Stuart Reston, earlier in the year to a heart attack, and her mother, Eloise Reston, years before that to colon cancer. Being without her own parents, Stefanie could very much relate to the pain of their absence in her life.

"Thanks for that." Bella smiled. "Doing my best to keep their dreams alive and make my own come true, to one degree or another."

Stefanie nodded, thinking of her own life and times. "It's really all any of us can ask for."

"So true." Bella eyed her perceptively. "What's wrong?"

After a moment or two, Stefanie answered straightforwardly, "A woman was found dead in the park…"

"What?" Bella cocked a brow. "Where?"

"On a trail by the river." Stefanie sighed. "I was the one who discovered her—naked and no longer breathing—"

"So what happened to her?" Bella asked anxiously. "Was it suicide? Drug related? Or something even worse…?"

"Honestly, I'm not sure," Stefanie responded. "That will be up to the police to determine. Or Detective Campbell Sawyer, more specifically." She pictured him in her mind and wondered if he would need her to come in for that formal statement. Or if they might meet again under more normal circumstances. "He's investigating the strange death."

Bella reacted to this. "Campbell… Figured as much."

"You two know each other?" Stefanie asked, but quickly realized this shouldn't come as a shock to her—assuming that the detective was a local, unlike herself.

"We know *of* each other, is more like it," Bella told her. "We both attended Reston Hills High School, but Campbell was a bit older, so we didn't hang out together or anything. But his father, Mason Sawyer, was also a police detective for the Reston Hills Police Department and was friends with my dad. Campbell decided to follow in his father's footsteps."

"Hmm…interesting." Stefanie fixed her face thoughtfully. "Sounds like someone else I know."

Bella laughed. "I suppose that some things do tend to run in the family, if the will is there."

"True. I just hope that Campbell—er, Detective Sawyer—can get to the bottom of what happened to that young woman…" Stefanie uttered, feeling regret over the life that had ended before its time.

"I'm sure he will," Bella said with confidence.

"Anyway, I'm heading home now. Not in the mood to stick around."

"I understand." Bella nodded her head. "Wish I wasn't obligated to do so, but someone needs to bring others up to date on what happened." She hugged her. "I'll call you."

"All right." Stefanie flashed her a tiny smile and walked off contemplatively.

She left the park in a blue Subaru Legacy sedan and drove down Hepmore Avenue for a couple of miles before turning left on Draker Drive. All the while, Stefanie couldn't get the image of the dead woman out of her mind.

What had happened to her? Could she have really been so strung out on drugs or whatever that she removed her own clothes and died? Or had her death been caused by someone else who had no qualms about having her discovered that way?

Maybe the answers would be forthcoming in short order with Campbell Sawyer on the case.

When she reached Meriotte Road, Stefanie swung left and was soon pulling up to her two-story, two-bedroom rented Craftsman home on a cul-de-sac that sat in front of a wooded area. She'd fallen in love with the place the moment she checked it out, feeling it suited her and reminded her of the house they'd had in San Antonio.

Stefanie stepped inside and onto white oak engineered hardwood flooring. She took a sweeping glance at the open-concept design, with vaulted ceilings and casement windows that offered an abundance of natural light. The ample living room had a stone fireplace and mid-century modern furniture with a separate, similarly furnished dining room. The amazing kitchen included a cozy breakfast nook, an island and quartz countertops. Though she loved making meals on the stainless steel gas cooktop and in the smart convection wall oven, she didn't do it often enough when cooking only for herself these days.

Her attention turned to the wooden U-shaped staircase as her Selkirk Rex cat, Curlie—with her dense cream, black and lavender coat of long hair—came bounding down the stairs. Stefanie knelt to greet her, and the cat leaped into her arms, clearly overjoyed to see her.

Or maybe it was her subtle way of saying she was hungry.

Stefanie decided it was a combination of the two, and chuckled. "Love you, too, Curlie." She petted her head and along the cat's back before setting her down. "Let's feed you," she said, noting that Curlie had already dashed off into the kitchen.

After putting high-protein wet cat food in a bowl and setting it on the floor, Stefanie watched Curlie devour it while she grabbed a bottle of water out of the black refrigerator, opened it and drank a generous amount.

Her thoughts turned again to the dead woman at the park and what may have been behind it—before she found herself pulling the flyer out of her pocket that she had never gotten around to discarding in the trash. Instead of doing so now, she stared at the brief info on the Braison Family. It seemed welcoming enough. And breathed life in its messaging instead of death. Maybe she would check it out sometime.

Stefanie took the flyer with her as she headed up the stairs to wash a load of clothes and make plans for the rest of her day, which had been altered unexpectedly by heartbreak.

CAMPBELL WAS, QUITE FRANKLY, left with more questions than answers after parting ways with the lovely Stefanie Nguyen. The celebratory mood of Founder's Day had dampened, for him at least, with the strange death of the as-yet-unnamed young woman. What circumstances had led to her ending up naked and dead in Reston Hills

Park? How long had she been deceased when her body was found? If her death wasn't self-inflicted, who had killed her? And did it have anything to do with the Braison Family cult?

Knowing he would need to exercise a little patience, Campbell took a proverbial chill pill as he drove away from the park. He would need to wait on the autopsy report to learn the exact cause of the woman's death, and pair that with any forensic evidence that might come from the Crime Scene Investigation Unit that had been dispatched to the scene and could offer some useful findings in the case.

In the meantime, Campbell turned his thoughts to the one who'd discovered the corpse. All he really knew at the moment about Stefanie was that she was relatively new in town—which explained how he'd managed to miss running into her at some point, as he would definitely have remembered if he had seen her before—and originally from San Antonio.

So how did she end up in Reston Hills? Was she there alone? He hadn't seen a ring on her finger. That didn't mean she wasn't hitched. Or without a romantic partner. Any local who was single, available and age compatible would be lucky to have her, if he were basing it on looks alone.

But even beyond that, from what little exchange they'd had, she seemed pretty cool under fire after seeing the dead woman on the trail. Stefanie had even expressed regret in not being able to prevent what had happened, as if she would ever have been able to do so.

It did make him even more curious about her. What was her occupation? He wondered if she could have been a psychologist or counselor, experienced in working with people in trouble. Or did her compassion just come naturally?

Maybe I'll get to ask her these things sometime—and more, Campbell told himself, more than willing to open up about himself in return should the opportunity present itself.

He pulled into the parking lot of the Reston Hills Police Department on Fourteenth Street. When he stepped inside the building, Campbell wasn't at all surprised to see that it was short-staffed, with much of the personnel out in the field. Or taking the day off.

That wasn't the case with Gloria Schecter, chief of police, who was in her office, busy on her laptop. She'd been around since his father was on the force, working her way through the ranks to her present position. She noticed him through the open blinds on her window, acknowledging him routinely with a nod before continuing what she was doing.

Campbell sat on a mid-back swivel chair at a wooden desk in his low-walled cubicle, where he did paperwork on his last investigation of a burglary ring. Juvenile offenders had targeted several local businesses before they were finally apprehended. Another case solved, but whether the perps could learn a lesson from this remained to be seen.

"Hey," Campbell heard a voice say.

He looked up at Detective Georgina Alvarez, who was in her forties, tall and slim, with dark blond hair in a pixie cut.

"Hey," he said. "Isn't this your day off?"

"I wish." She rolled her brown eyes. "Or maybe not. Ted had to work today, so I figured I might as well come in."

Ted Peñaflor was a deputy sheriff with the Eckerslin County Sheriff's Department and Georgina's longtime boyfriend. Whenever Campbell had broached the subject of marriage, Georgina, having once been stood up at the altar, had taken the position of not wanting to rock the boat. Or, in her words, *"If it ain't broken, why would I want to fix it—possibly ruining a good thing?"*

Campbell had hardly been able to argue the point, considering that his previous relationship with Naomi had ended before he could ever put a ring on her finger. Meaning that they probably would have ended up in divorce court. But that didn't deter him from wanting to get married—should someone come along who could put that fever in him.

Georgina was saying, "Just got through taking a statement from a woman who accused her on-and-off-again boyfriend of abusing her—and had the bruises to back it up."

Campbell frowned. "Is he in custody?"

"Not yet. He'd fled the scene by the time officers arrived." Georgina sighed. "He won't get far. We've got a BOLO out on his Ford Bronco Sport Big Bend."

"Good." Campbell hated the thought of any kind of domestic violence. "If he's guilty, he needs to answer for his actions."

"I agree wholeheartedly." She sat at her nearby desk. "Heard you're investigating a naked body found in Reston Hills Park…"

"Yeah." He paused and thought about Stefanie, who'd come upon the corpse. "The dead woman somehow ended up on a trail near the river. Unnamed, for the time being. The death could certainly be described as peculiar—given both the location and lack of any clothing or identifying materials in the vicinity."

"Hmm…" Georgina made a face. "Looks like you have your work cut out for you."

"What else is new?" Campbell tossed at her sardonically. "The answers will be forthcoming soon enough." His only real question at this point was just how satisfactory those answers would be. And where they might lead.

When his shift ended, Campbell headed out in his take-home vehicle. He lived in a two-story, four-bedroom modern farmhouse on Charliss Lane. He'd purchased the place when returning to Reston Hills three and a half years ago, getting a good deal on it from the previous owners. Sitting on three acres of pristine land, he envisioned a place to raise a family someday and enjoy each other's company.

After parking in the driveway in front of the two-car garage, Campbell left his vehicle and walked up to the house. Striding onto the covered porch, which had a natural wood porch swing, he unlocked the door and went inside.

The main floor had high ceilings, a spacious great room, formal dining room, den and primary bedroom—all set on parquet hardwood flooring, with double-hung windows covered by vinyl vertical blinds—with rustic hickory furniture. The gourmet kitchen had granite countertops, its own eating space and all the modern appliances for cooking. Upstairs were two nice-size furnished bedrooms with their own en suite bathrooms, and an extra room that was currently used for storage. There was a wraparound back deck, with lots of room to roam free on the grassy spaces.

Basically, it was everything Campbell could ask for

in a home. Well, almost. He wasn't particularly happy living all by his lonesome. Sharing the space with a significant other was high on his wish list. He imagined a beauty like Stefanie Nguyen would fit nicely here. First, he had to get to know her better and see if she was available and had any interest whatsoever in getting to know him—and take it from there.

Turning his thoughts to what to do for dinner, Campbell chose to take the easy way out and got on his cell phone to order a Philly cheesesteak pizza. It would go well with a bottle of beer that was in the side-by-side refrigerator. He could use the time to contemplate why a young woman would end up dead in Reston Hills Park on Founder's Day, of all days.

Chapter Three

The following morning, Campbell drove to work and was at his desk looking at his laptop as the forensic pathologist for the Eckerslin County Coroner's Office, Doctor Jennie Napier, appeared on the screen. In her mid-forties, she had blond hair in a blunt cut and green eyes behind square glasses.

Eager to hear the results on the unnamed dead woman, with the autopsy completed, Campbell asked, "What can you tell me about her?"

Jennie cleared her throat and said evenly, "Well, for starters, the death was a real tragedy, given that it was entirely preventable but happened anyway..." She took a breath. "The autopsy revealed that the decedent ingested a lethal amount of fentanyl that was mixed with carfentanil, a fentanyl analog—dying of acute fentanyl intoxication. The actual cause of death was fentanyl bromazolam—diazepam toxicity, to be exact."

"So, she died of a drug overdose?" Campbell said.

"Yes," Jennie responded surely.

"Self-administered?" he wondered. "Or, in other words, apart from whomever provided the fentanyl, could someone other than the decedent herself have given her the lethal dose deliberately?" He suspected the forensic pathologist would throw the ball back to his side of the court as the investigating police detective. He wanted to put it out there anyway to get her professional opinion.

Jennie remained poised as she answered. "Insofar as the overdose itself, the victim could have ingested the fentanyl voluntarily—or unknowing of the deadly consequences. But there's also good reason to believe that this wasn't an accidental overdose—"

Campbell cocked a brow. "Oh…?"

"There were cuts and abrasions on the decedent's arms, legs and feet, that had bloody blisters as well," she pointed out. "This would seem to indicate that she had been running while naked in the park in the wee hours of Founder's Day—as though away from someone, rather than haphazardly in a drug-abuse haze—hitting branches and shrubbery along the way. Before the fentanyl poisoning took its strongest effect and she lost consciousness, never to wake up."

"Meaning, we could be looking at outright murder," he said matter-of-factly. This included violations of Idaho state law regarding drug-induced homicide, making it a felony to supply fentanyl or any other illicit drugs that led to the death of a person. And federal law that involved the distributing of fentanyl that caused serious bodily injury and death of the victim.

Jennie pushed up her glasses. "That's something for you to determine conclusively, Detective," she told him. "But it does appear that the decedent may well have been fleeing for her life when she died—and, as such, was already doomed."

"That's one way to look at it," Campbell said, gazing at her. Another was that she'd taken a wrong turn, figuratively speaking, putting her on the path in life that could have still been survivable under other circumstances. Either way he sliced it, she'd died way too soon, and Campbell was intent on holding accountable the drug dealer or individual who'd ended the life of a young woman. "Was she sexually assaulted?" he asked.

Jennie shook her head. "There was no sign of a sexual assault."

"Okay." He had to ask, given the way the victim was found and how it could have been a factor in her death.

"Oh, something else caught my eye..." Jennie cut into his thoughts. "I couldn't help but notice that the decedent had the initials KB tattooed onto her right forearm. A boyfriend, perhaps?"

"Perhaps," Campbell went along for effect. He certainly couldn't rule out that the young woman might well have had a romantic relationship with cult leader Kenneth Braison. But the bigger question was whether or not he or his group had anything to do with her death. "We'll see about that and its relevance, if anything," Campbell told the forensic pathologist before ending the briefing.

CAMPBELL PULLED UP the digital case file from the department's Cold Case Unit on Lynda Boxleitner. Twenty years ago, in an investigation led by Detective Mason Sawyer, his father, the forty-one-year-old waitress and former cheerleader at Reston Hills High School was found dead and naked in Reston Hills Park on Founder's Day.

She had a broken nose, and there were other signs of physical duress.

But what had killed her was poison.

According to the Eckerslin County Coroner's Office,

Lynda Boxleitner had died from ingesting thallium sulfate, a highly toxic poisonous compound used primarily as an insecticide and rodenticide. Her death was ruled a homicide.

Campbell noted that she had been branded on her right forearm with the letters WB tattooed on it, which were said to be the initials for Wendell Braison, the then-leader of the Braison Family before it was eventually taken over by his son, Kenneth.

Though the elder Braison had long been thought to have been responsible for Lynda's death, Campbell's father had been unable to prove it, and Wendell Braison was never charged with killing her.

And neither was anyone else, Campbell thought, of the case that went as cold as ice. He gazed at the photograph of Lynda Boxleitner, whom his father had dated briefly in high school before meeting and falling in love with Campbell's mother, Alyssa. The picture was of Lynda in a cheerleader outfit from her younger years that showed off her voluptuous figure.

Though he didn't see any clear-cut physical similarities between Lynda Boxleitner and the still-unidentified woman killed at the park on Founder's Day twenty years later, given the similar circumstances that befell the women, Campbell couldn't help but wonder if the deaths weren't connected in some way. Perhaps the apple didn't fall far from the tree where it concerned Wendell Braison, who died seven years ago, his son Kenneth and murder.

I'll need to find out by paying the Braison Family compound a visit, Campbell told himself.

WITH HER HAIR in a high ponytail, Stefanie stood barefoot on a purple mat in the front of her studio on Haegadon

Lane for a power yoga class, wearing an orange crop tank and brown high-waist leggings. There were ten women in attendance for the physical and mental exercises, including Bella, who wore a red sports bra and white retro shorts on her toned, long-legged body.

With upbeat music playing, Stefanie took the lead in doing the intermediate routines, happy to lend her expertise to those in attendance. She was still reeling over finding the dead woman at the park yesterday, and could imagine her being part of the yoga class someday had her life not been extinguished.

"Call me anytime," Detective Campbell Sawyer had told her when handing her his card, with respect to the investigation.

I wonder if I should take him up on that? Stefanie asked herself, anxious to learn more about the poor woman's tragic death, as there had been no update on the case from the authorities. Apart from that, it would be nice to get to know the handsome detective—though she realized that might well mean discovering he was married with two children or engaged to the love of his life.

Stefanie frowned at the thought while refocusing on the yoga routines, which everyone seemed to be enjoying.

After the session ended, Bella, wiping perspiration from her brow with a towel, said, "Wow! That was a great workout, mind and body."

Stefanie smiled. "Glad you enjoyed it."

"What's not to like?" Bella grinned. "I'll have to give your tai chi class a try."

"You should," Stefanie encouraged her. "You'd be a natural."

"Hmm…maybe." Bella flung the towel over her shoulder. "Heard anything else about the dead woman in the park?"

"Not yet." Stefanie looked at her, knowing that she had the connections in town to get answers. "How about you?"

"Only that the autopsy has been completed, though the results haven't been released yet to the public." Bella wrinkled her nose. "Guess we'll know when we know how she died and what to make of it."

"True." Stefanie decided at that moment to take the plunge and give Campbell a call to see what he'd learned, for better or worse. She headed to the locker room, pulled her hair from the ponytail and hopped into the shower.

THE BRAISON FAMILY compound was located off South Petriss Road on around ten acres of rural land in an unincorporated area on the outskirts of Reston Hills. It consisted of one big ranch-style house and a number of cabins, where many members of the cult lived. Campbell wondered if this was where the OD victim had stayed before her death. And had someone there supplied her with the lethal fentanyl, making them complicit in the woman's demise?

As he walked past people—mostly in their twenties, thirties, and forties, but some children as well—who seemed almost oblivious to his presence, as though they'd been told to ignore outsiders, Campbell definitely felt out of place. Just as he was sure his father had been when visiting the same compound two decades ago in the pursuit of justice for the victim he was investigating.

Observing a gathering of people surrounding a man whom Campbell recognized as the cult leader, Kenneth Braison, he headed in that direction. He wanted to speak with the one person most likely to give him at least some of the answers he sought.

As his followers parted the way like sheep, Campbell walked up to the charismatic leader. In his early forties and with blue-gray eyes, Kenneth was a couple of inches taller and firmly built, with long, wavy brown hair combed backward, thick brows and a circle beard.

Kenneth brushed his long nose and said curtly, "Detective Sawyer... What brings you to my neck of the woods this time?"

Campbell peered at him and responded with an edge to his voice, "On Founder's Day, a woman was discovered in Reston Hills Park—dead from an overdose of fentanyl."

"Sorry to hear that," Kenneth uttered tonelessly. "Again, why are you here?"

"We think that she was part of the so-called Braison Family," Campbell replied bluntly. "As she was found naked and with no identification—apart from your initials tattooed on her right forearm—I need you to identify her..." Campbell watched Kenneth react to this before he took his cell phone out of his sport coat and pulled up a picture of the initials on the victim's arm. "Look familiar?"

"Yes, it does," Kenneth admitted. He added defensively, "We don't require anyone to do what she or he doesn't want to do. The initials are all about showing you're serious about being a part of our community and not here for games. That's it."

Campbell was sure there was pressure to capitulate, as a way to maintain control over his flock. "I'm not here for games," he pointed out sharply and then showed him a photo of the woman's face in death.

Kenneth took a long look at the decedent's face before sucking in a deep breath, then saying evenly, "Her name is Mia O'Dell."

Campbell took note of this. "How old was she?"

"Twenty-eight. Or so I was told."

"When was the last time you saw her?"

"A couple of days ago," he claimed.

Campbell set his jaw. "Did she live here?"

"Yeah, Mia stayed in one of the cabins when she chose to be at the compound."

Campbell peered at him. "Have any idea how she ended up at the park naked and strung out on drugs?"

Kenneth shrugged. "Wish I could say I did, but afraid not. There are no guards or gates keeping anyone locked in against their will—as opposed to keeping unwanted intruders out. So people tend to come and go as they please. It's better that way." He lowered his chin. "As to OD'ing on fentanyl, we do not use drugs here, Detective, as you discovered the last time we were graced with your presence. We have no control over what people choose to do away from the Braison Family ranch. Apparently, Mia decided to play by her own rules when she was elsewhere..."

"I think she was playing by the rules of whomever supplied her with the deadly fentanyl," Campbell countered straightforwardly.

"You could be right about that," Kenneth said. "But you won't find that person here. As I said, we don't allow drug use or dealing on this property."

"Wish I could simply take your word for that. But it doesn't work that way when investigating a homicide."

Kenneth flinched. "You said she OD'd..."

"She did," Campbell reiterated. "But whoever gave

Mia the drugs could be criminally liable for killing her—and won't get away with it."

"Nor should they," Kenneth said in agreement.

But he was too smug for Campbell's comfort. "Where were you in the early hours of Founder's Day?" he asked him directly, in corresponding with the estimated time of Mia's fentanyl exposure and death.

Kenneth answered quickly, "Right here—all night long and throughout the day. We celebrated Founder's Day here at the ranch." He paused. "Or most of the Family did."

"Can anyone vouch for this?" Campbell asked acutely.

"How about everyone?" Kenneth responded with ease. "We had a bonfire and sang songs. It was a real lovefest. Feel free to ask anyone."

Campbell doubted that any of his followers would contradict his alibi. Certainly not any who were still alive. Meaning that he likely wouldn't get very far in loosening any tongues if the man had drugged Mia. Or had taken or followed her to Reston Hills Park.

Campbell thought he might try a different tack. "You mind if I take a look around?"

"Not at all," Kenneth began, then added, "So long as you have a warrant. If not, then I do mind. This is private property, and we like to guard it like Fort Knox from any unreasonable intrusion. I'm sure you understand?"

Only too well, Campbell told himself. Braison was buying time for himself or others to cover any tracks that needed to be covered. That still didn't mean someone there was directly responsible for what happened to Mia O'Dell. But the resistance certainly caused his suspicious meter to shoot up.

"I'm sure I'll be back with the search warrant," he told him warningly.

Kenneth ran a hand across his mouth and glared. "Do what you must."

Campbell held his gaze. "I'll show myself out." He walked away and could feel all eyes on him as if he intended to break up their happy home. Only if there was good reason to. Like being responsible for one death. Or maybe two poisonous deaths crossing two long decades.

KENNETH BRAISON WATCHED intently as Detective Campbell Sawyer left the compound. He seemed full of himself. Just like his father, Mason Sawyer, who had once gone after Kenneth's own father, Wendell Braison. Decades ago, he had been accused of poisoning to death Lynda Boxleitner, a former member of the Braison Family. But the investigation had gone nowhere.

Though Kenneth had long suspected that his father had murdered Lynda—one of his then-lovers—after she had rebuffed his advances, he had denied this till his dying breath. Maybe he simply couldn't bring himself to come clean, not even to his only flesh-and-blood relative. Or maybe his father had been innocent after all and someone else inside the Braison Family, or outside of it, had killed Lynda for whatever reason.

Now Kenneth felt it was like déjà vu. Only this time, Mason Sawyer's son had all but accused him of killing Mia. Though they had slept together a few times, he had more action than he could handle and had no wish to end her life. Nor did he believe any other Family member would dare to do something without his permission that would damage its reputation. Much less, put them under the microscope again in a criminal investigation of that magnitude.

But then, even with his powerful position as the undisputed leader of the Braison Family, did that truly mean that someone hadn't decided to supply Mia with a life-ending drug? And if so, had her death been accidental? Or was there a reason why someone would have wanted her dead?

He headed to his residence for a moment or two of further contemplation, knowing he would need to gather everyone to share the unfortunate news of the unexpected passing of one of their own.

Chapter Four

Campbell was only too happy to invite Stefanie Nguyen for coffee at Harriette's Café after she called him for an update on the investigation. He would have preferred that she was calling with anything she may have remembered or learned regarding the death of Mia O'Dell. But if truth be told, he was willing to meet Stefanie under any circumstances to get to know her better.

Fortunately, she accepted his invitation. A good sign, perhaps. The fact that it happened to be an off day for Sarah Huffstetler was even better. Though Stefanie had absolutely nothing to worry about insofar as his being interested in Sarah, beyond their one date, he'd just as soon not have her serving them and suggesting there was something between them for Stefanie to chew on.

When she came into the café, he waved her over to the booth by the window, thinking that she was definitely a sight for sore eyes.

Standing, he grinned in greeting her. "Hey."

"Hi." Stefanie smiled back.

"Thanks for coming."

"No problem, Detective Sawyer," she said politely. "I had some free time, so…"

"Sit," Campbell told her, and watched as she slid into

one side of the booth, then he sat across from her. "Feel free to call me Campbell," he said, not wanting this to be formal, like an interrogation.

"Okay." She smiled. "So long as you call me Stefanie."

"I will." He smiled back, hoping he would get to use the name often.

Almost as if on cue, a short fortysomething waitress with a red shag haircut and round glasses came over with a pot of coffee, filling the two cups at their request.

After she left, Stefanie lifted her cup, took a sip and cut right to the chase, "So, where do things stand in the investigation—if I may ask? Did you find out who the woman is…?"

Campbell tasted his own coffee, having added cream, and responded, knowing it was all about to break, "Her name is Mia O'Dell. She was a local and twenty-eight. An autopsy revealed that she died as a result of fentanyl poisoning."

Stefanie's mouth opened, rueful. "That's awful."

"I know," he concurred. "Unfortunately, the drug epidemic in this country is very real. Even in a small town like Reston Hills, fentanyl use and abuse is a problem. In this case, the victim's fatal overdose, who gave her the fentanyl and how she wound up naked in the park are still under investigation." He didn't want to get too ahead of himself, but he felt that Stefanie, having discovered the body, deserved to be kept in the loop, at least to some extent. "Mia was a member of a local cult when she died…"

Stefanie lifted a brow. "You mean the Braison Family?"

Campbell looked at her with surprise. "You know about them?"

"Only what I've heard, which hasn't been much, really," she replied. "At the park yesterday, a member handed me a flyer while doing her best to prop up the group." She met his eyes. "You think they may have had something to do with her death?"

He sipped his coffee, musing. "It's entirely possible," he told her frankly. "So far, we have no proof that the fentanyl came from someone in the Braison Family. Or that the victim used it of her own accord, as opposed to with malice intent. Either way, you might want to stay away from their compound right now to be on the safe side."

"I understand." Stefanie sipped her coffee. "That's not really my type of thing," she told him.

"Good." Campbell didn't exactly mean to pass judgment on anyone who chose to align oneself with a cult. To each their own. But most who did were usually searching for some real meaning to life that might not yield the desired results. Especially if drugs were involved, along with the powers of persuasion that were misused. In this instance, he preferred not to have to compete for her attention with the likes of Kenneth Braison. Or, for that matter, any hot-blooded male who was attracted to her like he was.

Campbell couldn't help but wonder if he wasn't already too late to make a play for her affections. He decided it was best to ask in a roundabout way. "What brought you to Reston Hills?" Or was it who?

Stefanie stared at the question, her expression one of sadness. Then she said, maudlinly, "Two years ago, I lost my husband, Edward—a firefighter—after he was trapped in a wildfire that got totally out of control."

"I'm sorry to hear that." Campbell had nothing but deep respect for those who were willing to put their lives on the line to snuff out dangerous fires. Obviously, in this instance, it came at a high price.

"It was brutal for a while there," she admitted. "Being reminded of the life we had together—before any children could come along—was difficult, to say the least. Things got better over time." She took a breath. "Still, after a while, honestly, I felt I needed a change of pace. This seemed like a great location to make that change—so I sold my yoga and tai chi studio in San Antonio and opened a new one here."

I guess there's no one in her life at the moment, Campbell thought, figuring that after two years of being a widow, she might be ready to start dating again. "Glad you chose to make a home in Reston Hills," he told her, even if that optimism may have taken a hit after finding a dead body. He hoped that wouldn't make her want to flee at the first opportunity to do so.

"I have no regrets," she said, as if reading his mind. "Not counting what I stumbled upon yesterday. Sad as it was, I realize it could just as easily have happened in San Antonio—and, in fact, had more often than I care to admit, as drug addiction and overdoses were an issue there, too."

Campbell admired her courage and ability to put things in a proper perspective, difficult as that may be. "That is something that needs to be addressed nationwide," he told her. "But running from the problem and problems it creates is never the answer for any of us."

"I agree." Stefanie ran a hand through her hair, which was slightly damp, as if she had just showered. "So, I understand that police work runs in your family—"

"Yes, it does." He was surprised to hear her say that

and couldn't help but ask, curiously, "Have you been checking up on me…?"

"Of course not." She colored. "Bella Reston mentioned it to me yesterday at the park, after I told her you were investigating the woman's death."

"Bella…" Campbell sat back. "Why am I not surprised? Count on her to be the welcoming committee for newcomers."

Stefanie smiled. "She said you went to the same high school and that your father and hers were friends back in the day."

"The first part was true, though being a couple of years older than her, we didn't travel in the same circles, so to speak. As for the rest, I wouldn't exactly say that our fathers were friends. My dad did do some off-duty work for Bella's father from time to time, like extra security at one of his fundraisers or things like that."

"I see." Stefanie was thoughtful. "So, have you always worked for the Reston Hills Police Department?"

"Just for the last three and a half years," Campbell told her. "Before that, I worked as a detective for the Boise Police Department. Guess I wanted to spread my wings somewhat—even though I was inspired by my dad to go into law enforcement."

She angled her face to the right and asked inquisitively. "Why did you move back home, if you don't mind my asking?"

"I don't." He rubbed his chin and contemplated the question. "It was due to a combination of too much stress on the job, too little return on my efforts, a failed relationship and homesickness." Campbell gazed into his empty cup. "Also, it gave me the chance to get closer to my father, which hadn't always been the case since my mother's death years earlier."

Stefanie gave him a knowing look. "I lost my own parents when I was just a teenager, but cherish all the time that I had with them. I'm glad you took the opportunity to bond with your father while you still could."

"Me too." Campbell found himself liking her more and more with each passing moment. If it were strictly up to him, he could sit there talking with her all day—and even into the night. But he was still on duty and sure she had other things on her plate to do. "Well, I won't take up any more of your time today," he said reluctantly.

"And I shouldn't take up any more of yours," she said with a straight look.

Believe me, I don't mind one bit, Campbell told himself, but responded, "Glad I was able to let you know where things stand at the moment in the investigation."

"So am I." She offered him a smile.

After paying for the coffee, he walked her to her car, where Campbell said tentatively, "Maybe we could do this again sometime?"

Stefanie nodded. "Works for me."

"Okay." He hoped that would be sooner rather than later, but wouldn't push it just yet.

She got into her Subaru Legacy, started it and drove out of the parking lot.

Campbell followed suit in his own vehicle, trailing for a bit before turning in a different direction at an intersection. He wondered where things could go between them, allowing his imagination to run wild for a moment or two, before coming back down to earth. Then he turned his attention to the ill-timed death of Mia O'Dell and the circumstances that may have led up to it. What might his father have to say about this, given the almost eerie similarities to a case he'd investigated twenty years ago?

Stefanie drove down Pickford Street, away from Harriette's Café, glancing up at the rearview mirror to see that Campbell's car was no longer there, as if his vehicle had disappeared into thin air. She almost wished he had followed her home, and they could have talked some more. Apart from getting the scoop on what his investigation had uncovered on Mia O'Dell's death, Stefanie welcomed the conversation beyond that unsettling news. It had been a while since she had opened up like that to a man, and she felt good about this. The fact that he had indicated an interest in seeing each other again, while not necessarily in relation to police work, was something she was totally amenable to. She wanted a full life in Reston Hills, beyond her yoga studio and hanging with Bella. Now was the time to push forward with that and see where she landed.

After pulling up to her house, she went inside and was greeted by Curlie. "Hey, you," Stefanie said, chuckling as the cat lifted it paws onto the leg of her boot-cut jeans. "Looks like you've missed me. Well, back at you."

Picking her up, Stefanie kissed the cat on the top of her head, which Curlie evidently enjoyed. Or at least the attention.

Stefanie fed her and left her alone, while she walked into the living room and took out her cell phone. After sitting on a gray mid-century-modern accent chair, she called Bella for a video chat, wanting to fill her in on the latest in case she hadn't heard.

Bella accepted the chat and said cheerfully, "Hey."

"Hey." Stefanie kept a serious look on her face. "Got a sec?"

"Yes, I'm all yours. What's up?"

"I just met with Detective Sawyer… Campbell," Stefanie told her.

Bella's eyes widened. "Really?"

"Yes, we had coffee at Harriette's Café while he provided an update on the case."

"I see." Bella narrowed her gaze. "What did he say?"

"The woman's name is Mia O'Dell," Stefanie told her.

"What?" Bella looked shocked. "Mia…?"

"I take it you knew her?" Stefanie said, based on the reaction.

"She used to work for my father as his housekeeper," Bella pointed out. "We weren't close or anything, but I'd see her in town every now and then." She sighed. "Now she's dead. How?"

"Drug overdose," Stefanie told her. "Campbell said that she died from fentanyl poisoning."

"That's terrible." Bella's brow furrowed. "Didn't realize she was into that."

"She may not have been," Stefanie pointed out. "Campbell's investigating how she came to have the fentanyl in her system and if the death was accidental or deliberate."

Bella reacted, a thin brow shooting up. "He thinks someone could have intentionally caused Mia to OD on fentanyl?"

"Possibly. Or otherwise played a part in her ending up naked, alone and dead in the park." Stefanie took a breath. "Apparently, Mia was involved with the Braison Family cult. Are you familiar with them?"

"Yes," Bella answered matter-of-factly and as a local

historian. "They've been around these parts for decades—started by a controversial and charismatic man named Wendell Braison—attracting those most susceptible to life outside the mainstream. As far as I'm aware, they haven't caused much trouble, apart from occasional skirmishes with the law, and don't seem to be a hot bed for drug activity. But then, what do I know?"

She became thoughtful, prompting Stefanie to ask curiously, "What?"

Bella licked her lips and answered, "Well, I do seem to recall years ago when another woman who belonged to the cult was found dead at the park—on Founder's Day, of all things. I'm sketchy on the details, but I don't believe the case was ever solved..."

"Hmm." Stefanie found that intriguing. What were the odds? "Coincidence?"

"What else could it be?" Bella offered. "Just popped into my head. Let's see if Campbell can reach the right conclusions in the death of Mia O'Dell."

"Agreed." Stefanie had a sense that he would. She could only hope that Mia's fatal drug overdose wasn't nefarious in intent.

After disconnecting from the video chat, Stefanie pondered the tragedy while also wondering if the Braison Family could have been behind it. Or were they truly harmless for the most part, as Bella had suggested?

Maybe I need to see for myself, Stefanie thought. If only to put her mind at ease in feeling a kinship of sorts to Mia, whom she'd happened upon, as though to help her rest in peace, if at all possible.

Chapter Five

Campbell drove down the dirt road off Saldnon Street till reaching his father's horse ranch in Fallon's Creek, Idaho, some twenty miles from Reston Hills. After leaving the police force nearly a decade ago following his wife's death, Mason Sawyer bought the one-hundred-and-seventy-five-acre private property, east of the Caribou-Targhee National Forest. There, he raised American quarter horses, Appaloosas, and Percherons, offered trail rides, and seemed at peace.

Or at least, that was how Campbell saw it as he pulled up in front of the main house behind his father's black Land Rover Range Rover Evoque and a red Hyundai Tucson hybrid that belonged to his longtime girlfriend, Sally Panettiere. He hadn't been able to bring himself to marry again.

Standing in the driveway, Campbell watched as his father and Sally rode up to him on their horses.

Mason Sawyer was in his early sixties and had gray hair in a flow cut and a horseshoe mustache. With his work on the ranch and weightlifting, he had managed to stay in shape since his days on the force. Touching the wide brim of his off-white suede cowboy hat, Mason peered at Campbell through blue eyes and said tonelessly, "This is a surprise."

"Guess I should've called," Campbell admitted, but he felt that this was something that needed to be discussed in person. So he took his chances. He regarded Sally, a book editor, who was in her late fifties, slender and hazel-eyed, with a blond shullet haircut, wearing an almond-colored straw cowgirl hat. "Hey, Sally."

"Hey to you, Campbell." She showed her teeth. "Believe me, your dad's just as happy to see you as I am."

"She's right," Mason said, leaving no doubt. "You're always welcome here, surprise or not."

"Thanks." Campbell grinned, comforted with the thought but still wishing he had texted him first. He gazed at his father and asked, "Can we talk?"

"Sure," Mason told him. "We'll put the horses in the stables and meet you inside."

"Okay." Campbell watched as they rode off, then he headed for the house. He had a key but rarely used it, preferring not to intrude if uninvited. In this instance, he had his father's permission.

The spacious ranch house was amid mature chokecherry trees with a pond nearby. He unlocked the door and went inside, looking at the open-layout with lots of windows and Western style furnishings on plank flooring. It was the type of place his mother would have loved, had she lived long enough to see it.

But life didn't always work in ways that were understandable. He got that. At least his dad had found a way to move on, and with someone who made him happy in her own right. Just as his mother had.

Twenty minutes later, Campbell was sitting on the

back porch with Mason on Adirondack chairs. Both were drinking fresh lemonade that Sally made for them. Resting on the floor, as if with nothing better to do, was Mason's dog, a male yellow Labrador retriever named Hopper.

After a moment or two, Campbell got to the point when he said, "I'm working on a case involving a young woman named Mia O'Dell, who died on Founder's Day from fentanyl poisoning."

"Hadn't heard," Mason said. "Sorry for her."

"So am I." Campbell looked at him. "She was found in Reston Hills Park—naked. The initials KB were tattooed on her right forearm. I was able to establish that they were short for Kenneth Braison, the current leader of the Braison Family cult—"

"Really?" Mason tasted the lemonade as his expression grew more distraught. "Interesting…"

"I had the same reaction, all things considered," Campbell admitted. "I took a look at the cold case that you investigated twenty years ago involving the death of Lynda Boxleitner. The similarities were uncanny, right down to the tattooed initials WB on her forearm—albeit, which were short for Wendell Braison, Kenneth Braison's father. I couldn't help but wonder if the two deaths could be connected in one way or another?"

Mason's brow furrowed. "Two decades is a long time, son."

"But not so long that a killer couldn't have hung around from one murder to let history repeat itself, for whatever reason," Campbell suggested, even if he knew it would be a hard sell. Even for himself.

"I suppose." His father brought the glass of lemonade

to his mouth. "One problem with that theory is that Wendell Braison, the chief suspect in the murder of Lynda Boxleitner, died seven plus years ago. Though I was never quite able to nail him, no one else surfaced to the degree that I came to believe I had targeted the wrong man. So unless Wendell found a way to rise from the dead, there's no way he could have been responsible for the latest death. Besides that, Lynda died from thallium sulfate poisoning, as opposed to fentanyl that you say Mia O'Dell OD'd on. Lynda's death was ruled a definite homicide. Apparently, that wasn't the case with Mia's. Doesn't seem to add up."

Though he agreed at face value, Campbell said, "Clearly, Wendell Braison did not kill Mia. But maybe his son picked up where he left off—right down to all but staging Mia's naked body at the park on Founder's Day to practically mimic the death of Lynda Boxleitner. As for fatally poisoning the victim with fentanyl mixed with the fentanyl analog, carfentanil, instead of thallium sulfate, it could be mainly a matter of accessibility. Go with what you have—in abundance these days for practically anyone who wishes to obtain it on the black market. Though the coroner didn't outright declare the death a homicide, she might as well have. Aside from going after the drug dealer for supplying the fatal dose of fentanyl, cuts and abrasions on the victim's arms, legs, and feet indicate that there's a good possibility she was trying to get away from whomever may have given her the drug, as though in fear of her life. That amounts to murder, in my book." *Or close enough to warrant a serious investigation into the death*, he told himself, sipping the lemonade.

Mason jutted his chin. "Have to admit, it smells

fishy—the whole thing." He paused. "I assume you've questioned Kenneth Braison?"

"Yes, I questioned him," Campbell verified.

"And...?"

"And the jury's still out on that," he told his father. "Braison apparently has an alibi for the estimated time of Mia's death. But given that those in his inner circle will likely say whatever he tells them to, I'm not ready just yet to see that as the gospel—till we can get into the compound, where Mia was staying, with a search warrant. It's also more than possible that if Kenneth Braison was the one pulling the strings in killing her, it wouldn't have been difficult to get someone else to do his bidding as a loyal soldier for the cause."

"I suppose." Mason ran a hand across the dog's head. "If the Braison Family is behind both deaths—a generational murder pack of sorts—I hope you can succeed in piecing together where I fell short."

"So do I." Campbell eyed his strained profile. "But for the record, you investigated the Boxleitner murder to the best of your ability with what you had to work with, Dad. No one still around today on the force faults you for being unable to solve the case. Unfortunately, cold cases are a part of law enforcement across the country. Hell, even around the world. We can't solve them all—even if we wanted to."

"You're right about that," Mason said, with a catch to his voice. "Somehow, though—strange as it sounds all these years later—I felt as if I let Lynda down in not being able to allow her the dignity of being able to rest in peace."

"Doesn't sound strange at all," Campbell said. "You and Lynda dated once, giving you a reason to take what happened to her personally on some level. Just as we both had to deal with some things when Mom died—though the cause of her death was quite different." He drew a breath. "Maybe my investigation can make things right for you with Lynda. Or at least give those close to Mia some closure."

Mason pinched the bridge of his nose. "I appreciate that, son. About your mother, too, whom I loved dearly, just as you did—and still miss very much."

"Same here," Campbell told him.

"I kept some info from my investigation," Mason said. "I'll go through it and see if anything comes up that may be of use to you in your case—"

"Okay." Campbell finished off the drink, happy to have his help. He hoped to return the favor by making a more concerted effort to visit the ranch more often, now that he was a resident of Reston Hills again. "I'd better go," he told him, getting to his feet.

Mason nodded. "I'll walk you out."

Campbell grinned at his childhood memories. He'd loved spending as much time as possible with his dad, and those moments had seemed like they would last forever. Till his mother passed and everything seemed to change. Now they were back on the right track, more or less, and trying to start building new memories.

MASON STOOD NEXT to Hopper as they watched Campbell drive off. Having Lynda Boxleitner's strange death brought back to the surface had thrown him for a loop, as he digested what his son had come there to say. The fact that another woman had died pretty much the same way and was left naked in the park like trash was disturbing, to say the least. Having it occur on Founder's Day was all the more troubling.

What was up with that?

Was someone trying to tell him something? Perhaps Lynda or even Wendell Braison—from the grave—wanted to show there was a real connection between the past and present that couldn't be ignored?

Had Kenneth Braison truly decided to walk in his father's shoes, killing one of his followers that he considered uncooperative? Someone threatening the cult's very existence?

Can I really find the answers to Lynda's unfortunate death that have eluded me for over twenty years with the help of my son? Mason asked himself. Or did one death really have nothing to do with the other? He wondered what he had missed and if it could ever turn back the hands of time in delivering justice for Lynda, who didn't deserve to have her life ended that way.

It occurred to Mason that perhaps he had been looking in the wrong direction by going after Wendell. Maybe the same was true for Campbell as he focused on Kenneth Braison. Maybe someone else was the true enemy and was intent on throwing them off the trail.

Or maybe they were definitely on the right track with the Braison Family and only needed to make their case.

When he heard the front door open, Mason turned and saw Sally walk out toward him. Hopper ran up to her.

Sally had a worried look on her face as she regarded Mason and asked him, "Everything all right?"

He thought about it, wanting to just give a pat answer. But knowing how much she had come to mean to him as his partner in life and the closest thing Campbell had to a mother with Alyssa no longer in the picture, Mason regarded his girlfriend and responded truthfully, "Not so much, really. But maybe it can be."

"How?" she asked ill at ease.

He put his arm around her shoulders and replied, "I'll explain inside..."

STEFANIE WASN'T QUITE sure what to expect when she drove through the gates and into the Braison Family compound. Was it a mistake to go there and try to get a read on presumably the last place that Mia O'Dell had spent her final hours prior to ending up at Reston Hills Park? *Maybe I should leave the sleuthing up to Campbell and the police department*, Stefanie thought. Then she half joked to herself, *What fun would that be?*

Truthfully, she considered this anything but an exercise in fun and frolic. Beyond that, she would just have to play it by ear.

After parking, Stefanie exited the car and was met by Jasmine and a tall, brawny Hispanic man in his thirties with a bald head and crooked nose.

"Greetings," Jasmine said spiritedly. "Stefanie, right?"

"Yes, good memory," Stefanie told her, considering all the people she must regularly try to recruit.

"I make it my business to remember anyone I get a good vibe from," she said sincerely, and looked at the man. "This is Juan."

Stefanie smiled. "Hi."

He didn't smile back, as if resistant to any outsiders. "Hello," he said stiffly.

"Anyway, I wanted to take you up on the invite, Jasmine," Stefanie told her, "and check out the place."

Jasmine beamed. "I'm so glad you did."

"Me too," Stefanie said hastily as she gazed at the stone-faced Juan.

Jasmine took her hand and said, "Come, let me show you around..."

"Okay," Stefanie agreed, watching Juan head off in another direction but still peering at her.

Jasmine noticed and said, "Don't pay any attention to him. He's naturally suspicious of anyone who wants to see what we're all about, as though we're supposed to be closed off to expanding our tent. That isn't the case at all," she argued.

"Cool." Stefanie smiled. She had no intention of joining the cult, but she was most interested in what she could learn about Mia.

After being led around the open country space that included fruit trees, crops and farm animals for a self-sustaining lifestyle, Jasmine introduced Stefanie to a few of the members, then took her to a cabin.

"This is where I live," Jasmine said proudly.

Stefanie took a sweeping glance around the cozy cabin with bamboo flooring and wicker furniture. "Nice," she told her.

"I try to make it as comfortable as possible."

Stefanie smiled softly. "Do you know Mia O'Dell?" she asked evenly.

"Yes, Mia's part of the Braison Family," Jasmine said. "Are you friends with her?"

She doesn't seem to know what happened to Mia, Stefanie thought. *I have to tell her.*

But before she could, a tall and fit bearded man with

presence walked into the cabin, and Jasmine said, with eyes wide with admiration, "Kenneth—"

"Hey." He regarded her with a serious look, then turned to Stefanie and said, "I'm Kenneth Braison."

The head of the Braison Family, Stefanie deduced by his commanding presence. "Stefanie Nguyen."

Kenneth shook her hand. "Nice to meet you, Stefanie."

"You too," she told him politely.

"I trust that you've been made to feel welcome to our little slice of paradise?"

"Yes." Stefanie flashed a smile. "Thanks to Jasmine." She looked at her and got a grin in return.

Kenneth fixed his eyes to Jasmine's face and told her intently, "Everyone's meeting in the courtyard in five minutes."

She nodded. "All right."

All three left the cabin, where Juan was waiting outside. Kenneth eyed Stefanie and said succinctly, "Hope you'll come again. Juan will show you out..."

Stefanie glanced at Juan and understood that this was Kenneth's way of telling her it was time to leave, whether she was ready to or not. She looked at Jasmine, who seemed confused, but didn't dare voice an objection. Nor did Stefanie wish for her to put herself at any risk. Especially after what had happened to Mia. Or perhaps because of it.

After leaving the compound, Stefanie wondered if Campbell might be up for having dinner with her. There was only one way to find out.

KENNETH SENSED THAT Stefanie Nguyen was on a fishing expedition rather than truly being interested in becoming part of their family. He'd heard through the grapevine that she was the one who found Mia in the park. So, was she visiting the compound on behalf of Campbell Sawyer, to see if he could connect her death to the Braison Family? Or was it a personal quest by Stefanie to see what rocks she could overturn for her own curiosity?

Either way, Kenneth was not about to let the group his father started be torn apart. Not as he was now the head of the Family. That included making sure that Stefanie stayed in her own lane—as a yoga instructor, he'd learned—if she knew what was good for her.

With everyone now gathered before him, Kenneth sucked in a deep breath and said, with the appropriate remorse, "I have some news to share with you… It's with a heavy heart that I just learned that one of our own, Mia O'Dell, died on Founder's Day from a drug overdose." He watched for a moment as the expected moans and murmurs came from his flock. "She was found in Reston Hills Park. Though I'm sure this comes as a shock to most of you, given that drug use is strictly prohibited on these grounds, Mia may have fallen in with the wrong crowd outside of our reach…and paid the price…"

Kenneth saw this as an opportunity to further separate the Braison Family from outside influences and their decidedly negative play on human nature. If this made them stronger, then all the better. He could only hope that Mia's death wouldn't make its way back to him and everything he stood for. Just as his father had before him.

Chapter Six

"Do you like Vietnamese food?" Stefanie asked Campbell over the phone. Not that it was the extent of what she liked to cook, but it seemed like a nice way to go for starters, if he was interested. But she was also open to other types of meals she was good at making.

"I like every type of food," he said diplomatically.

Good answer, she thought, and asked him, "Would you like to have dinner with me tonight?"

Without pause, Campbell said surely, "I'd love to."

"Terrific. Does seven o'clock work for you?"

"Yes, seven is good."

"Okay." Stefanie thought about Curlie. "By the way, you aren't allergic to cats, are you?"

"Not at all," he said, then added, "Love cats."

She chuckled. "Good."

Stefanie texted him her address while inside her car in the parking lot of a grocery store, where she would need to pick up a few items for dinner now that it had been confirmed.

Two hours later, she had prepared lemongrass chicken thighs, red rice and Vietnamese egg rolls called Cha Gio, to go with white wine and taro rice pudding for dessert.

Hope he likes it, Stefanie told herself after freshening

up. She changed into a floral peach-colored midi shirt-dress and slipped on wedge espadrilles.

Campbell arrived right on time, grinning as he came in. "You look great," he told her at the door.

"Thanks." Stefanie gave him a once-over, noting that he was wearing a yellow oxford dress shirt, dark gray wool slacks and black loafers. "You clean up pretty nicely yourself."

He laughed. "It's nice to have a reason to every now and then."

"That goes both ways," she admitted, inviting him inside.

Her cat wasted no time cozying up to Campbell's pant leg, as if reuniting with an old friend.

Stephanie said, "This is Curlie."

"Hi, Curlie." Campbell allowed the cat to run around him playfully before scooting off. He looked around. "Nice place you have here."

"Thanks." She smiled softly.

He took a whiff of the food and stated, "Smells wonderful."

"It'll taste even better." Stefanie felt confident enough to be presumptuous in this instance. Till proven otherwise.

"I have no doubt," he told her coolly. "Can I help with anything?"

"You can pour the wine, if you like," she replied, pointing out the brown Shaker-style cabinets where the wineglasses were kept.

"Will do."

As Campbell did that, Stefanie put out the food on the

mid-century round wooden dining room table. They sat across from each other on brown faux leather side chairs.

"Delicious," Campbell declared, the moment he bit into a lemongrass chicken thigh.

Stefanie giggled. "Good to know." *Guess I haven't lost my touch after all*, she told herself pleasingly. After he commended her on more of the food, she said to him, "I went to the Braison Family compound this afternoon..."

"Really?" A thick disapproving brow shot up.

She felt the need to explain. "I needed to have a look at where Mia spent her time before what happened to her. And since Bella felt it wasn't a threatening environment for me to be overly concerned about, I went, hoping to get more insight into the life Mia led."

"I see." He scooped up some red rice onto his fork. "And how did you make out on your journey?"

"Not very well, I'm afraid." Stefanie sliced her knife into the Cha Gio. "Before I could make any headway at all with Jasmine—the one who gave me the flyer at the park—Kenneth Braison cut that short. He had a muscular man named Juan escort me off the premises. I don't think it was something I said. Or maybe I didn't say enough to be considered worthy of being a potential member of the Family."

"It was likely neither of those," Campbell told her frankly, forking up a piece of chicken. "I'm guessing that Braison, as the cult leader, is being extra cautious as to who he lets in, while having to look over his shoulder as we investigate the death of Mia O'Dell."

Stefanie angled her face. "So, you still think he may have something to do with it?"

"I certainly can't rule it out at this stage, even if the

man can apparently account for his whereabouts when she died." Campbell sat back, pensive. "Wouldn't be the first time a Braison has been at the center of a mystery surrounding a woman found dead in Reston Hills Park on Founder's Day."

Stefanie sipped her wine thoughtfully and said, "Bella mentioned something to me about that. But she didn't provide any details. Are you saying that Wendell Braison, Kenneth's father, was suspected of killing another cult member?"

"Yeah," Campbell said matter-of-factly. "Twenty years ago, a forty-one-year-old waitress and Braison Family member named Lynda Boxleitner was left in the nude at the park, after ingesting a lethal amount of a poison called thallium sulfate. Wendell Braison, who was thought to be romantically involved with Lynda—his initials, WB, were tattooed on her arm—was the chief suspect in her death. But it was never proven. The case has remained in limbo ever since. Though Braison has been dead himself for years now, this story has continued to haunt Reston Hills like a curse."

Stefanie peered at him. "You seem to know a lot about the case…"

Campbell nodded while holding his wineglass. "My father, Mason Sawyer, was the lead detective in the investigation," he told her. "He also happened to have been acquainted with the victim, having dated Lynda years earlier when they were both in high school." Campbell tasted the wine. "Dad did everything he could to find out who killed her and why, but came up short. It was probably the one unsolved case that has stuck with him to this day."

Stefanie took a breath. "If the Braison Family was behind both deaths, do you think it could have been part of a generational ritual?" She had read about this type of thing with other cults and devil worshippers—often involving animals as sacrifices. Could they have taken it much further here, with humans being targeted as sacrificial lambs?

"The thought has crossed my mind," Campbell answered. "But given the twenty years between the deaths, it's more likely that they are linked either by kinship—making the killings personal in nature—or possibly a copycat killer emulating a decades-old murder to carry out another today. At this point, all options are on the table."

"I expected as much," Stefanie said, feeling she may have gotten carried away in her theorizing as a layperson. She dabbed a napkin at the corners of her mouth. She only wanted to see Mia's death solved. If Campbell could solve his father's case as well, then two birds could be killed with one stone, to both of their satisfactions. "Speaking of the table, are you ready for dessert? I made taro rice pudding."

He grinned. "Yes, I've saved enough room in my stomach to take on your pudding. Have at it. I'll help clear the table and refill the wineglasses."

"Okay." She was starting to like him more with each passing moment and wondered what else might be in store for them.

CAMPBELL HAD TO admit that he could get used to having dinner and dessert with Stefanie in a hurry. Sure beat eating alone, as he'd been doing way too often since returning to Reston Hills. The fact that she was a great cook made it that much more enjoyable. To say nothing of just how lovely she was to be around. He liked Stefanie's finicky cat, too, as she'd seemed to take to him just as quickly.

They took their wine goblets with them while sitting on a blue chenille upholstered sofa in the living room.

"So, have you dated much since living in Reston Hills?" Campbell had to ask, even if for selfish reasons.

Stefanie tasted her wine. "Haven't dated at all since moving here," she admitted. "Too busy with other things and lack of interest, I guess." She gazed at him. "Unless you call this a date?"

He didn't hesitate to do just that. "I hope we can call this a date. I'd like that to be the case."

She grinned. "So would I."

"Then that's that." Campbell grinned back at her, seeing this as a positive step in getting to know one another.

Stefanie regarded him. "You mentioned having a failed relationship when you were living in Boise. What happened there?" she probed curiously.

Campbell considered this. He didn't want to keep anything bottled up inside him that could take away from a readiness to move on. "Her name is Naomi Espelita," he said levelly. "Naomi had a lot going for her, including a career as a successful classical musician. Unfortunately, we weren't right for each other. Too little common ground and not enough willingness to meet each other halfway. I wish nothing but the best for her—just not with me."

"Okay." Stefanie let that sink in for a moment. "Do you ever want to get married—if the right person comes along? And have children?"

"Yes, to both," Campbell answered without hesitation. "I'm a big believer in marriage, kids, the whole nine yards. If that right person comes along, I'm there—all the way…"

Her teeth shone. "Nice to know."

"What about you?" Figured he might as well satisfy his own curiosity while they were at it. "Could you see yourself marrying again? And starting a family?"

Stefanie took a sip of wine and met his gaze squarely. "Yes, absolutely. I never asked to be a young widow—but it happened. If a second chance comes along to be a wife again and a mother, I would certainly take it and hope things would work out."

"Okay." Campbell nodded. He wanted to kiss her so badly in that moment but instead talked about what they enjoyed doing outside work. While he mentioned working out at the gym, traveling, reading and riding horses, her hobbies included swimming, watching reality television shows and surfing social media sites. They both liked to jog and hike.

Before he could come back to that desired kiss, Stefanie asked him boldly, "Do you mind if I kiss you?"

Campbell could barely contain his enthusiasm. "Not in the slightest."

They leaned in to each other and exchanged a soft but steady kiss. Though feeling aroused and enjoying the feel of her mouth upon his, Campbell kept his libido in check. He wanted to make sure this was what they both wanted before going further.

"Nice," he murmured after the kiss ended.

"Yes, it was," she seconded with a smile. He left it at that, with visions of more to come.

When Stefanie walked him to the door a few minutes later, Campbell said, "Thanks for dinner."

She blushed. "Thanks for coming."

"Next time, I'd like to return the favor by cooking you a meal," he told her.

"So, you cook, too?" Her eyes lit up. "Hmm... Man of many talents, huh?"

"Something like that," Campbell teased her.

"Then it's a date."

"Okay." He grinned at her.

As he drove away from her house, Campbell felt more than grateful that they'd met at all, though he wished it had been under better circumstances. The last thing he wished upon anyone was to find a dead body—no matter the circumstances. But Stefanie had done just that and taken an interest in Mia O'Dell and her affiliation with the Braison Family. Even if Bella Reston, her friend and a prominent member of Reston Hills society, apparently dismissed the cult as a threat, Campbell was far from convinced. Especially after his father's ordeal in being unable to connect the dots in going after Wendell Braison years ago.

Maybe the more things changed, the more they remained the same. Meaning that Kenneth Braison still had to be considered a person of interest in Mia's death, just as his father was in the death of Lynda Boxleitner.

As such, Campbell felt a professional obligation to protect Stefanie, over and beyond his romantic interest in her, so long as the current investigation remained active. But he wouldn't overstep his bounds in dictating whom she chose to associate with—even if it was members of the Braison Family.

Chapter Seven

At eleven a.m. the following day, Campbell sat at the counter in Harriette's Café beside Detective Georgina Alvarez while they awaited the judicial go-ahead to search the Braison Family compound.

Sarah Huffstetler came up to them with the coffeepot, filling their cups. Ignoring Georgina, she said to Campbell in a syrupy voice, "Hey, handsome."

"Good morning, Sarah," he said to her evenly.

"Heard you were here yesterday with a pretty lady. Anyone I know?"

"I doubt it." *Word travels fast in a small town*, Campbell lamented. He hoped she wouldn't make a scene. "Just a friend," he said tonelessly, even if he was starting to see far greater possibilities with Stefanie.

"We all need friends around here, right?" Georgina threw out with amusement.

Sarah shrugged. "If you say so." She gazed at Campbell. "If things don't work out with your friend, you have my number."

He nodded. "Got it." *I deleted your number right after our one date*, he told himself.

After she left, Georgina chuckled and said, "Looks

like someone has the hots for you, Campbell. Or maybe more than one woman..."

"Nothing going on with me and Sarah," he emphasized. "We went out once and that was it."

"Not sure she realizes that."

"She'll come to terms with it sooner or later." Campbell added some cream and sipped his coffee.

"So who is this other *friend*, Sawyer?" Georgina teased him. "Have you been holding out on us while jumping back into the dating game?"

"Not really." Campbell laughed. "Her name's Stefanie. Met her on Founder's Day at the park."

Georgina cocked a brow. "When?"

"She was the one who discovered Mia O'Dell's body on the trail," he explained, then paused. "We hit it off."

"I see." Georgina grinned. "Good for you. Hope this one is a keeper, just like with me and Ted."

"That would be great," Campbell had to admit, knowing that she and her deputy sheriff boyfriend worked. Though they were apparently not interested in marriage—to each their own. While wedding bells weren't exactly on the docket right now between him and Stefanie, the fact that both were open-minded in that regard could bode well in the future.

Georgina sipped her coffee with two sugars, then asked, "So, do you think we'll find anything incriminating at the Braison Family compound related to O'Dell's death?"

Campbell weighed this. "One can only hope so," he replied, adding more cream to his coffee. "If there's anything at all at the compound in the way of fentanyl or other evidence that can somehow tie Kenneth Braison or one of his followers to Mia's fatal overdose, we'll find it."

"Maybe. Based on past run-ins with Braison, I'm betting that if the Braison Family was involved in her death, they probably covered their tracks well."

Just as Wendell Braison apparently did in managing to skirt the law and his father in the death of Lynda Boxleitner, Campbell told himself. "Our job is to uncover any proverbial tracks if they lead anywhere, or to someone," he countered. "Maybe it's the drug dealer who gave Mia the deadly fentanyl indifferently. Or perhaps she was killed deliberately to keep her from spilling the beans on something or someone who preferred that it went with Mia right to the grave."

Georgina nodded and said, "Let's hope we can give her the peace she deserves—even if she made some bad choices and couldn't pull herself out. If this was out-and-out murder, all the more reason to get whoever was responsible—so no one else has to die."

"Yeah, you've got that right." Campbell tasted the coffee. He couldn't help but wonder if such an unsub could have played a role in Lynda Boxleitner's murder. Could Kenneth Braison have actually killed her instead of his father? Kenneth would have been in his early twenties when she died. Making him more than old enough to have done the deed—either for himself or on behalf of Wendell Braison.

But Dad never mentioned Kenneth as a suspect in Lynda's murder, Campbell told himself. So maybe he hadn't killed her. But that didn't let him off the hook for involvement in Mia's OD death.

When his cell phone rang, Campbell lifted it from the

pocket of his blazer and answered, listening to the caller. After disconnecting, he told Georgina, "We got the search warrant. Let's go pay the Braison Family a visit—"

"I'm with you," she said eagerly before they finished off their coffees, paid for them and left the café.

THAT AFTERNOON, STEFANIE sat poolside on a turquoise chaise longue chair beside Bella as they sipped on cocktails while wearing bathing suits in anticipation of a dip in Bella's resort-like saltwater pool. After her father's death, Bella had inherited and moved into his enormous house—which, to Stefanie, was probably the most elegant home in town—that he in turn had inherited from his father, Malcolm Reston, whom it had been passed on to by his own father, Arthur Reston, the town's namesake.

Stefanie was still reeling from kissing Campbell. She had prompted the kiss, surprising even herself. But it felt like the right time, with the right person. So she'd thrown caution to the wind and gone for it, hoping he wouldn't embarrass her by turning down the request.

Thank goodness he welcomed the invite and was a great kisser, as I suspected, Stefanie thought in her reverie. They'd already made tentative plans for another dinner date, this time at his place. She was excited at the prospect of furthering what they had started.

Stefanie refocused on Bella, who was talking animatedly about the next big project that she was spearheading.

"The Annual Reston Hills Charitable Gala this Saturday will raise money for local theater programs, literacy initiatives and the arts," she said enthusiastically. "It will also be lots of fun with live music, performances, an auction, lots of food and more…"

"I look forward to attending," Stefanie told her while wondering if she could invite Campbell as her guest. Or would he be too busy working on one case or another? That could be something she would simply have to get used to were they to become a bona fide couple. "Maybe I'll even bid on something at the auction—all for a good cause."

Bella laughed. "Or not. Whatever works. You'll definitely be on the VIP list as a good friend—and feel free to bring anyone you want…" She gave her a teasing look. "I'm just saying."

"Thanks for that." Stefanie showed her teeth while making plans to bring Campbell along for the ride. "Can't wait." In the meantime, she could only hope that Campbell and his colleagues wouldn't be left with more dead bodies to deal with. "So, Campbell's looking into whether Mia's death was in any way connected to the unsolved death of Lynda Boxleitner—the member of the Braison Family you mentioned who was found murdered twenty years ago in Reston Hills Park on Founder's Day."

"Really?" Bella batted her lashes. "Seems like a stretch after so many years, but what do I know? Tell me more."

"Afraid I don't have much to tell," Stefanie admitted, flexing her toes. "Only that Campbell's dad, Mason Sawyer, who investigated Lynda's death, found that she, too, was left naked at the park with the initials of Wendell Braison tattooed on her arm and had been fatally poisoned—albeit with a different type of poison than what Mia OD'd on. But since Mia had Kenneth Braison's initials tattooed on her arm and died under similar circumstances, I suppose it's only natural that Campbell would want to see if the father and son could have perpetrated the poisonings for whatever reason as the leaders of the Braison Family…"

Bella sipped her drink. "Well, when you put it that way, it does seem like a good idea for Campbell and the police department to check out if there's any way that Wendell and Kenneth could've used their power to dispose of cult women they viewed as threats to their organization."

Stefanie leaned toward her. "Yeah, as weird as it sounds, I suppose anything's possible till proven otherwise. I'd at least like to see Mia's death solved, for obvious reasons, as the one who found her."

"I'm with you there," Bella said flatly. "As my dad's former housekeeper, Mia deserves justice in any way she can get it. Just as Lynda Boxleitner does. Never too late."

"I agree." Stefanie was hardly an expert on cold cases. Or even hot ones, for that matter. But she sensed that with Campbell investigating the two deaths, anything was possible. She put the cocktail glass to her lips before tossing out casually, "So, I invited Campbell over for dinner last night…"

"Oh, really?" Bella flashed her an exaggerated shocked look. "Didn't see that coming."

"Neither did I, to tell you the truth," Stefanie said before tasting her drink. "But we've gotten to know each other a bit. He seems like a great guy with an interesting background—and someone that, if it continues, could be a good fit for me at this stage of my life."

"Well said." Bella grinned at her. "I say go for it. Campbell and I never connected that way, but I think he's a great catch and so are you, girlfriend. He's lucky to catch your eye—and maybe your heart over time—"

"Hmm…" Stefanie liked the sound of that. "I was thinking the same thing," she said with a laugh.

Bella frowned. "Now, if only I can land the man of my dreams—after my ex, Jeff, turned out to be a dud—or at least someone who can hold my attention more than the blink of an eye."

"I'm sure that will happen sooner or later," Stefanie told her sincerely. "Look at you, you're the complete package. What man wouldn't want to be by your side and all that accompanies that? You just have to be willing to let someone—*the one*—in."

Bella chuckled. "How poetic. You're right, of course. We'll see how it goes. Maybe my knight in shining armor will await me at the Annual Reston Hills Charitable Gala."

"Maybe." Stefanie smiled, wondering if Campbell would prove to be her own knight in shining armor when all was said and done.

Bella suddenly got to her feet, wearing an apple-red halter tankini, and said, "I don't know about you, but I'm ready for a swim."

"Me too," Stefanie told her with a smile. Before she could lift up, wearing a green-and-white cap-sleeve one-piece swimsuit, Bella had already dived into the pool. Stefanie followed her, jumping into the water, anxious to put her swimming skills to work.

CAMPBELL AND GEORGINA arrived at the Braison Family compound, along with additional armed members of the Reston Hills Police Department and a K-9 unit that included drug detection canines, to execute a search warrant on the premises.

They were met at the gate by two men. One Campbell recognized as Juan Barrientos, Kenneth Braison's top sidekick, having encountered resistance from Barrientos during a previous encounter at the compound. The other man was African American, in his thirties and just as muscular, with black hair styled in cornrows and a Garibaldi beard.

Campbell walked up to the men, presented the search warrant and said, "Now, if you'll kindly step aside and let us do our work, we can be in and out in no time flat." *Or longer, if we find reason to stick around for a while*, he thought.

Barrientos gazed at the search warrant, glared at him and said to the other man resignedly, "Let them through."

They both stepped aside as Campbell and Georgina led the way inside the compound, where everyone spread out, while looking specifically for any illegal drugs or weapons on the premises. Of particular interest was the presence of illegally manufactured fentanyl or IMFs, or the detection of fentanyl analogs, such as carfentanil. As well as any evidence they came upon that suggested that Mia O'Dell's death had begun at the compound before ending in Reston Hills Park.

When Campbell approached Kenneth Braison—or actually, more the other way around—the cult leader's forehead was creased in three places as he muttered, "You're back again…"

"I'm sure that doesn't come as a surprise," Campbell shot back. "I told you we'd return with a search warrant, which Juan Barrientos got the first look at." He handed the warrant to Kenneth. "Now it's your turn."

Kenneth barely glanced at it. He sneered at Campbell and said, "Go ahead, look wherever you like. We have nothing to hide. You won't find anything, Detective," he said confidently.

Campbell retorted, "We'll see about that."

"Yeah, right," he said mockingly.

Campbell peered at him. "Mind showing me which cabin Mia O'Dell was staying in before she died?"

"I'll be happy to take you to it," Kenneth replied. "I instructed everyone to leave everything as it was. Wouldn't want you to think we'd tampered with evidence or anything."

Yeah, I bet, Campbell thought as he followed him while directing a K-9 team to join them.

When they arrived at the cabin, Campbell asked Kenneth to wait outside as the search for evidence ensued.

To Campbell, the cabin where Mia had supposedly lived alone was almost too tidy to be believed, leading him to suspect that any potential evidence may have been tampered with. They went through the motions nonetheless, hoping to get lucky.

"Find anything?" Campbell asked the K-9 handler.

Sergeant Vivienne Olmstead, fiftysomething with auburn hair in a flip bob, tightly held the leash of her German shepherd/Belgian Malinois mix canine partner, and said ruefully, "Nothing. No drugs detected whatsoever. At least not inside the cabin."

"All right." Campbell was wearing nitrile gloves as he did his own search through the cabin, with its wicker furniture and standard household items—coming up empty with anything that could tie solidly to the commission of a crime.

Outside, he met up with Georgina, who had the same

results. "We haven't come up with any illicit drugs or illegal firearms," she said stiffly.

Campbell frowned. "Looks like they cleared out anything that might come back to bite them," he reasoned, similar to his previous search for drugs and drug paraphernalia that had yielded no positive results. "We'll have to see if we can connect any outside drug traffickers to the Braison Family."

Georgina nodded. "As well as ask around to try and learn who Mia may have been hanging out with inside or away from the compound that may have something to say about what she was up to the day she died."

"Yeah," Campbell concurred, wondering to what extent, if any, the Braison Family was behind the death.

They checked out more places, spoke to a few of the followers—none of whom seemed willing to say much on or off the record—and rendezvoused with the rest of the team, before deciding there was nothing more to do there at the moment.

As they were leaving, Kenneth and his sidekick Juan walked up to them.

Kenneth regarded Campbell and said gloatingly, "I take it you found nothing of use to you, Detective, while searching for answers in Mia's death?"

"Not yet." Campbell jutted his chin, knowing this was precisely what the cult leader had anticipated. "Doesn't mean we won't stop trying."

Kenneth responded, "As you should. Believe me, I'd like to know how Mia ended up OD'ing as much as you. The Braison Family isn't a haven for drugs or drug use—and we wouldn't stand for putting that poison into our bodies."

"If you say so," Campbell said sarcastically.

"I do." Kenneth sighed. "It was the same when my father was at the helm of the Family and *your* father was trying to put the squeeze on an innocent man when another cult member fell prey to poison being put into her system. Wishing for something to be true doesn't mean it is—"

Campbell glared at him, knowing Kenneth had managed to get under his skin by bringing his father into the current case. As well as reminding him about the failure to get the evidence needed to charge Wendell Braison with murder.

Maybe you won't be so lucky when this is over, Campbell thought, and walked away from the cult leader and a hard-nosed Juan Barrientos.

Outside the compound, Georgina pouted and said, "Braison's a real piece of work."

"And probably a lot worse," Campbell told her. "Whether or not that rises to the level of cold-blooded killer remains to be seen." No matter his dislike of the man, he wouldn't jump the gun by indicting him without the hard evidence to prove his case. *Any more than my dad was willing to do when going after Kenneth's father, even if it meant letting the case grow ice cold*, Campbell told himself as they headed for his vehicle.

KENNETH WATCHED FROM behind the gate as Detectives Sawyer and Alvarez drove off, along with other law enforcement personnel. He hated that they had invaded his territory like they owned the place. But, as expected, they had come up empty-handed. This didn't mean they had gone away for good. As long as Mia's death remained unsolved, the cops figured to be a problem.

"What do you think?" Juan asked, ill at ease, as they walked back inside the compound.

Kenneth ran a hand across his mouth thoughtfully. "I think we need to tread carefully," he answered. "With Mia dead and fingers pointed in our direction, we have to stand strong and not allow them to break up everything my father worked so hard to achieve."

"That won't happen," Juan assured him. "They have nothing, and we have each other. The Braison Family is solid enough to push back anything the police can try to drum up against us."

"I'm glad we're on the same page."

"Always."

Kenneth smiled, putting a hand on his shoulder. "You're a good soldier for the cause, Juan."

"I try my best," he told him.

That would have to be enough, as far as Kenneth was concerned. As was the case for every member of the Family. It was the outside influences that most concerned him. The same ones who may have been responsible for Mia losing her way.

Assuming there wasn't one or more traitors within their midst, deliberately breaking the rules in a misguided attempt to stop the movement. And everything that it stood for.

Chapter Eight

The following day, Campbell drove down tree-lined Pughten Road and onto the luxury waterfront estate of Bella Reston, who, he had to admit, played her part admirably in her family legacy by playing up the core values of the town that bore her great-grandfather Arthur Reston's name.

As Stuart Reston was Mia O'Dell's last known employer—apparently before she became a member of the Braison Family—it seemed a good place for Campbell to start to get some further insight into Mia's life before being recruited and, apparently, indoctrinated by the cult.

Beyond that, as Bella was friends with Stefanie, Campbell thought it was a good thing to win Bella's support in his bid to become closer to Stefanie than he had to anyone in a long time. *I'm sure Bella wants Stefanie to be happy in Reston Hills if I can provide some of that happiness*, he told himself.

He got out of the car, parked not far from Bella's blue metallic BMW X7 M60i SUV outside a four-car garage. *At least I know she's home*, Campbell thought with a grin.

Walking up to the massive two-story brick house with loads of architectural windows, a big swimming pool in the backyard and in a wooded setting, he recalled coming there once as a boy with his dad. Seemed like a place one could only dream of. But his dreams did not go that far at the time.

Or now, for that matter.

The current version of himself realized that it took more than the size of a house to make a home—if the other aspects failed to fall in place properly. Apparently, that wasn't a problem for Bella, having returned to her childhood home with the death of her father four months ago as a single woman after divorcing her husband. Or was it the other way around? The way he'd heard it, Jeff Lacombe, the ex, whom Bella had met in high school, had cheated on her, and that had ended the marriage, with Jeff and his new girlfriend relocating to New Mexico.

Not my problem, Campbell told himself, sure that with all Bella had to offer, she would have no trouble finding someone else to share her life with—just not him. Assuming that wasn't already the case.

After ringing the bell, the door opened and Bella's housekeeper stood there. The thirtysomething medium-size woman with short and curly brunette hair asked, "Can I help you?"

Taking out his badge, Campbell answered, "I need to speak with Ms. Reston," remembering that Bella had reclaimed her maiden name following the divorce.

"Come in," the housekeeper said tonelessly.

Campbell walked into a long hall with marble tile and framed family photographs, and past bifurcated stairs, before being led to the great room and asked to wait. He glanced around at the traditional furnishings, floor-to-ceiling windows and an exposed-brick wood-burning fireplace.

"Hello."

He heard the familiar pleasant voice and turned to face Bella, who smiled.

"Campbell…or should I call you Detective Sawyer?"

He grinned. "Campbell is fine." Especially since he didn't want this to seem like an interrogation so much as an informal chat between old acquaintances, if not friends.

"All right." Bella walked up to him, wearing a sleeveless black wide-leg jumpsuit and flats. "Nice to see you, Campbell. How's your dad?"

"He's doing well, thanks." Campbell appreciated that she asked, remembering that he'd done some work for her father.

She smiled. "So, what brings you my way?"

"Mind if we sit?" he asked, meeting her green eyes.

"Of course. Where are my manners?" Bella eyed a set of maroon Chesterfield chairs angled toward one another by an oval glass table. "Sit."

Campbell sat down and waited for her to do the same before getting right to it. "As I'm sure you're aware, we're investigating the suspicious death of Mia O'Dell."

Bella gave a nod. "Yes, I'm totally aware of that—thanks, in part, to our mutual friend, Stefanie, who's been filling me in on any news she picked up on it. How does any of this relate to me?"

"It doesn't, in so many words," he told her. "But it does your late father, Stuart Reston, albeit indirectly…"

Bella batted her lashes. "I'm afraid I don't follow…"

Campbell explained, "As far as we're aware, Mia's last-known employer was Stuart, who employed her as a housekeeper. We're backtracking her life to try and understand how Mia ended up dead in the park on Founder's Day. Can you tell me anything about her working for your father?"

Bella took a breath and said evenly, "Not too much. I wasn't living in the house at the time. What I do know is that she was his housekeeper for a few months before he died—seemed as though Daddy had trouble keeping help that lived up to his standards—before he caught her stealing and fired her."

"Really?" Campbell asked attentively.

"That's what I was told," she said, smoothing a brow. "Apparently, it wasn't the first time she stole from him."

"Did he say what she stole or tried to steal?"

"Some of my late mother's jewelry, which he refused to part with." Bella ran a hand through her hair, which stayed remarkably in place. "As well as money that he often had lying around haphazardly."

Campbell leaned toward her chair. "Did your father ever report any of this to the police?" If so, he could easily look it up for more details.

"No, I don't think so. My dad was a private person and preferred not to get the police involved if at all possible." Bella folded her arms. "He chose instead to simply fire Mia. Feeling she was let off easy, she went on her way without a fuss."

"I see." Campbell scratched his jaw. "Had you seen Mia since she was fired?"

Bella met his gaze. "I spotted her on occasion in town—but we never spoke."

"Did your father ever indicate to you any knowledge that Mia was using drugs?"

"No. But I think if he had ever suspected this, Daddy

would almost certainly have fired her on those grounds alone." Bella frowned. "As my late mother got addicted to painkillers while battling cancer, my father understood what drugs could do to you. He would never have tolerated substance abuse from one of his employees."

Campbell understood this. He flashed back to his own mother and her courageous battle with breast cancer to no avail. Even with the prescription drugs used to control the pain, they never seemed to be enough, and his mother's suffering really only let up at the end of her journey. He and his father couldn't help but find solace that she was finally at peace—even while missing her more than they could once express properly to one another. Campbell imagined the same was true for Stuart Reston and Bella.

Regarding her, Campbell asked, "Do you have any idea what motivated Mia to join the Braison Family?"

Bella pondered the question, then responded speculatively, "I can only assume that perhaps she was susceptible to their messaging and Kenneth Braison's powers of persuasion. Beyond that, using and abusing fentanyl—before or after—may have weakened her resistance that much more."

"You're probably right on both counts." Campbell still wasn't sure if someone from Braison's orbit—including Kenneth himself—had given Mia the deadly fentanyl. Or if it was someone on the outside. "I don't suppose you would know if Mia was seeing anyone when she worked for your father?"

"Sorry. Can't help you there." Bella pursed her lips. "I hardly spoke to Mia when visiting my dad, and he never mentioned her having a boyfriend, girlfriend or whatever."

"Okay." From what they had come up with thus far, it did appear that Mia was not romantically involved with anyone. At least not outside the Braison Family. But they were still looking into cell phone records that might provide more clues into her final days.

Bella eyed him and said inquisitively, "So, Stefanie mentioned that you were looking into whether there might be a Braison Family connection between Mia's death and the death of the woman at the park on Founder's Day twenty years ago."

"That's true." He didn't deny it, knowing she was around then to remember what had to be big news in Reston Hills on that of all days. "There are some similarities between what happened to Mia and Lynda Boxleitner two decades ago that bear checking out."

She cocked a brow. "I know that Wendell Braison was once considered a suspect in that Founder's Day murder. If he really killed her, do you honestly think Kenneth Braison could have followed his lead in killing Mia as another member of the Braison Family? Why would he do that?"

"People kill for all types of reasons," Campbell pointed out matter-of-factly. "Some are more complicated than others. Some less. Could be that the Braisons felt empowered to do as they pleased to protect what was theirs. Even to the point of murder, albeit decades apart. If neither Braison had anything to do with the deaths, then we'll look elsewhere. Until then, they both will continue to be persons of interest here." *Probably said more than I needed to*, Campbell thought, but somehow felt that she understood, having a vested interest in solving both deaths, if at all possible.

Bella made a face. "If the Braisons were behind the fatal poisoning of *two* innocent women and you're able to prove it, I certainly hope they get what's coming to them. No one should have to die like that. Especially if it was part of a warped cult act of revenge or as some sort of human sacrifice."

"I couldn't agree more about the tragic manner in which they died." Campbell drew a breath. "Time will tell if there is some symmetry here that ties the father to the son—or the Braison Family itself to one or both deaths."

She nodded. "As the sole representative of the Reston family legacy, I do hope you can do right by the town in putting at least Mia's death to rest, if not Lynda Boxleitner's."

"I'll do my best," he promised, then added, to lighten the mood a little, "No pressure, right?"

"Not from me." Bella smiled. "I'm sure you have enough of that from others."

Campbell grinned, welcoming her pressure-free support. He supposed that the most pressure he felt right now, he put upon himself. As his father had before him. He fixed his gaze to her face and said, "Thanks for the chat. I'd better let you get back to your day."

They stood and walked to the front door, where Bella stated, "I'm glad you stopped by, Campbell." She looked at him with a soft smile. "I was hoping to catch up with you and see how the case was coming along—seeing that Stefanie wound up being part of the investigation, as she found Mia's body."

Campbell jutted his chin. "Yeah, that was unfortunate. But it gave me the opportunity to meet Stefanie, who's strong enough to weather what she went through and continue to fit in the community."

"Thanks, in part, to you," Bella told him. "She really likes you, which I'm sure you already know."

"Yeah." Campbell blushed. "I think it works both ways."

"Good to know. Stefanie's heart is in the right place. She deserves a second opportunity to experience love—if it comes her way..."

"Don't we all." He wondered if she was experiencing this again herself with anyone. Or still waiting for the right person to come along, with her busy life and all.

Once inside his SUV, Campbell pondered just how long it would take for real love to develop between him and Stefanie. Patience was something he was good at and clearly this was true for her as well.

The rest would have to work itself out.

JASMINE ROXBURGH HESITATED as she approached the ranch house Kenneth lived in with his latest girlfriend, Siobhan Froggatt. Siobhan was from London, England, and had been drawn to the Braison Family ever since arriving in the States two years ago, finally working her way to Kenneth's bed when he tired of his prior bedmate—whom Jasmine suspected had been Mia O'Dell.

Now Mia was dead from a drug overdose, and the Braison Family, after a few parting words from Kenneth, seemed to be going about its business as though she was yesterday's news and no longer pertinent to speak about further.

But more troubling to Jasmine was how Mia, whom she'd considered a friend and not a drug user, came to have fentanyl in her system. Did she get it from someone inside the compound? What did Kenneth know that he was keeping from the police?

Jasmine considered the search by the authorities that came up empty yesterday. It went as expected, with Kenneth and Juan seeing to it that anything they had to cause suspicion—including loaded weapons—was well hidden. She'd wanted to speak to Detective Sawyer, but was too afraid to even try, with eyes everywhere and anywhere.

Then there was Stefanie, with whom Jasmine felt a kinship. Jasmine had learned that she was the one to discover Mia's body. Was that what had brought Stefanie to the compound, before Kenneth sent her away?

Jasmine knocked on the front door, and a follower named Eva opened it. In her early twenties and rail thin with long, stringy blond hair and big blue eyes, Eva asked, "Are you looking for Kenneth?"

"Yes," Jasmine said, second-guessing if it was truly a good idea to approach him directly about Mia.

"Come in." Eva smiled at her. "He's in his office with Siobhan and Juan."

"All right." Jasmine walked alongside Eva on dark hardwood flooring and past farmhouse furnishings in an open-concept layout, knowing that there was never any wandering around the house alone unless you were part of Kenneth's inner circle, which she wasn't.

Eva knocked on the door, and a voice gave her permission to open it. She looked at Jasmine and said, ill at ease, "You can go in now." Eva added, as if feeling it might be needed, "Good luck."

Jasmine smiled softly at her, replying, "Thanks."

When she walked into the big office, which had a large

picture window and wooden furniture, Jasmine spotted the three people huddled around each other conspiratorially.

Kenneth broke away and approached her. He asked in a friendly tone, "How can I help you, Jasmine?"

"I was wondering if I could talk to you about Mia?" Jasmine replied tentatively.

"Of course." He looked over his shoulder at Juan and Siobhan, who was a dark-haired, dark-eyed beauty in her mid-twenties, tall and shapely, and told them, "Leave us."

Juan glared and Siobhan pouted as they walked past her. Once they were out of the office, closing the door behind them, Kenneth peered at Jasmine and asked with an edge to his voice, "So, what's on your mind?"

Jasmine suddenly felt tongue-tied as she contemplated where to go from here.

Chapter Nine

In his home office, Mason Sawyer sat on a well-worn, high-backed black leather ergonomic chair at an L-shaped walnut desk that had a small filing cabinet attached to it. His dog, Hopper, sat lazily nearby, rejecting the opportunity to roam free on the ranch.

Spread across the desk were case files from his investigation into the murder of Lynda Boxleitner two decades ago. Though he'd stepped away from police work since retiring—after an injury and his wife Alyssa's death made it too difficult to remain on the force—Mason had never quite been able to rid himself of information on Lynda's mysterious death. It was as though, deep down inside, he believed that he might need to come back to it again once the case was reopened.

He wasn't sure if that was official or not, but Mason believed that his son was hell-bent on clearing up his present-day death of Mia O'Dell by poisoning case in conjunction with the cold case death of Lynda Boxleitner.

Mason felt obliged to do his part to the extent he could as a retiree. He thought, *It's the least I can do in trying to help Campbell piece this together, if the deaths were connected at all.* Not to mention having another crack at solving Lynda's murder long after the fact—once and for all.

But as of yet, he saw nothing while going over the investigation notes, witnesses, evidence and whatnot that he hadn't seen twenty years ago.

All roads still seemed to lead back to Wendell Braison as the most likely culprit in Lynda's death. But that hadn't been nearly enough to make an arrest, much less get a conviction and prison sentence.

But what if I'd been wrong in pursuing Wendell? Mason asked himself, lifting a can of beer and taking a sip. What about Kenneth Braison? Had he overlooked him? Though Kenneth was twentysomething at the time and fully capable of killing Lynda, his alibi of being in Boise when the murder took place had held up. On the other hand, Wendell—who was thought to have been romantically linked to Lynda and manipulative in controlling her and his other followers—was sketchy in his own alibi. But did that make him guilty of murder?

And could Kenneth have pulled a fast one by faking his whereabouts at the time of Lynda's death?

What am I missing? Mason mused, going through the files again. Could another Braison Family member be at the center of both deaths?

Or were Lynda and Mia's poisoning not connected by time? And perpetrated by one or more persons outside of the Family?

When Hopper suddenly got to his feet, Mason snapped out of his reverie as Sally entered the office. She was carrying a plate of oatmeal cookies, his favorite, and said, "Thought you could use a break with some fresh-baked cookies…"

Mason grinned. "That, I could." He watched as the

dog ran up to her, seeking to get a cookie or two himself. "Looks like Hopper feels the same."

"I guess he does." Sally smiled while tossing the dog a cookie, which he caught in midair. She sat the plate on the desk in an empty spot. "So, how are we doing here?"

Mason almost hated to say *not so good*. He had filled her in on what was happening after Campbell paid them a visit. She had been nothing but supportive in his desire to assist his son in reopening the investigation that came with his biggest regret as a police detective.

"Still a work in progress," he settled on telling her. "Could be that I'm only spinning my wheels, going nowhere fast. But it's just as possible that there may be something here that could be a means to one end or another—"

Sally seemed amenable to whichever way this went, kissing the top of his head. Mason was left to wonder if he could ever be satisfied with never knowing who ended Lynda's life—or why?

STEFANIE WAS IN her studio giving tai chi lessons to a group of children. She had once been one of those children in her youth, with her parents encouraging her to develop skills in the ancient Chinese meditative martial art. She hoped to one day teach her own children tai chi, assuming she were so blessed to become a mother someday. The thought of Campbell being the perfect father of those children entered Stefanie's head, making her tingle, though such a possibility was way too soon to get too out in front of.

She came back to reality for now as Stefanie went through warmups with her class of eager learners. This was followed by tai chi short forms, then breathing exercises, or chi kung, while lying down.

The goal, for both children and adults, was to improve conditioning aerobically, balance and flexibility, and upper- and lower-body muscle strength.

She was satisfied that this was happening and the participants—or in this instance, their parents—were getting their money's worth.

Just as the class had come to an end and the children—wearing white tai chi uniforms like her own—began filing out to their waiting parents, Stefanie was surprised to see Bella strut into the studio. For an instant, she wondered if Bella had thought that it was an adult class today but got her timing wrong. However, as she wasn't exactly dressed for exercise and had designer sunglasses on the top of her head, Stefanie assumed Bella was only stopping by because she happened to be in the area.

Still, Stefanie couldn't help but say jokingly to her, "Here for some beginner tai chi?"

Bella laughed. "Not quite." She flipped back her hair. "Just came from a meeting and thought I'd come by to say guess who paid me a visit earlier today?"

"Uh..." From the look on her face, Stefanie guessed who it might be. But said instead, "Your ex, hoping to somehow win you back?"

"Only in his dreams." Her curly lashes fluttered frivolously. "Actually, it was your boyfriend."

"Campbell?" The name popped out quite naturally, though Stefanie didn't exactly think of him as her boyfriend at this point.

"The one and only," Bella told her, hand resting on a slender hip.

"We're not official right now," Stefanie had to say, though they seemed to be headed in the right direction. She eyed her curiously. "So why did Campbell come to see you?"

"It wasn't to arrest me or anything." Bella chuckled. "He came to talk about Mia O'Dell, who worked for my father as his housekeeper."

"Right." Stefanie was thoughtful. "I remember you saying that."

"Basically, Campbell just wanted to know what I knew about Mia during that time—including possible drug use—and even afterwards when she joined the Braison Family." Bella sighed. "I told him that my father caught Mia stealing and fired her. But I knew nothing about her taking fentanyl, for how long or who gave her the deadly drug. Or, for that matter, how she became indoctrinated by a cult."

"Hmm…" Stefanie wiped her face with a towel. She was surprised that Mia had been a thief. But what did she really know about her, other than that Mia OD'd on fentanyl and was part of the Braison Family? "I'm sure that anything you were able to tell Campbell was helpful in providing clarity to Mia's life, leading up to her death."

"I hope so. But actually, it worked both ways," Bella told her. "Since I had his attention, it gave me an opportunity to pick Campbell's brain on his thoughts about a possible connection between Mia's death and that of Lynda Boxleitner twenty years ago."

"Oh, really?" Stefanie said, regarding her pensively.

"Campbell made a compelling argument that there may have been a link by bloodline and the cult to the two deaths." Bella narrowed her eyes. "I told him that if this proves to be true, then he should certainly do everything he can to bring whoever was responsible to justice. If that boils down to only Kenneth Braison because his father Wendell Braison is dead, then so be it."

"I agree with you there," Stefanie said, wondering if the Braisons were behind one or both deaths. Or were there other culprits responsible?

Bella looked at her and stated, "By the way, we talked about you, too."

"Me?" Stefanie batted her lashes with surprise.

"Basically, we both agreed that you're a lovely, wonderful person who deserves a second chance at love, wherever it may be and with whom—him, for instance."

Stefanie colored. "Thanks for the show of support." *And thank you, too, Campbell, for seeming to really care for me.*

"Anytime." Bella showed her teeth. "I know you'd stick up for me were the shoe on the other foot."

"Absolutely," she assured her. "Well, I'd better jump in the shower. I'll catch you later."

"All right." Bella pulled the sunglasses down and over her eyes. "I still want to learn tai chi one of these days."

"Whenever you like," Stefanie promised with a smile before heading for the locker room, thinking about Campbell and where things could go between them.

CAMPBELL WALKED INTO the office of Police Chief Gloria Schecter. Pushing sixty, she was slim in her uniform and had ash-blond hair in a piecey pixie cut. She had been a lieutenant when his father worked in the department and served as his boss.

Sitting in a brown leather chair at an adjustable-height

corner desk, Gloria looked at him through oval glasses with blue eyes and said levelly, "Detective Sawyer…"

"Chief." Campbell took a couple of steps forward. "As you know, I'm looking into the Mia O'Dell death on Founder's Day."

"Yes—she OD'd, right?"

"Yeah," he responded, "and may have been helped—over and beyond tracking down the dealer—"

"Uh, okay…" Gloria sat back. "So, where are we in the investigation?"

Campbell regarded her. "I'm checking out the possibility that Mia's death could be connected to the death of Lynda Boxleitner twenty years ago, which my father was investigating."

Gloria leaned forward, interest piqued. "Are you, now?"

"Both were found naked at the park on Founder's Day, poisoned to death, and with a tattoo on their right forearm that bore the initials of the Braison Family leaders—Wendell Braison and Kenneth Braison, accordingly." Campbell took the liberty of sitting on an armless fabric guest chair across from the desk, then continued, "Since you were my dad's lieutenant then, I was wondering if there's anything you can remember about the Lynda Boxleitner homicide case that might help with the investigation?"

Gloria pushed up her glasses thoughtfully and replied, "I assume you've spoken with Mason about this?"

"Yeah, we've talked," Campbell confirmed. "He's told me what he remembered and is digging through some old files on the case. I've also checked with the Cold Case Unit and am looking to see if anything clicks."

Gloria drew a breath and said deliberately, "I remember when Lynda Boxleitner was dumped at the park, after having been fatally poisoned and disrobed by presumably her killer. We investigated the homicide thoroughly, led by Mason—Detective Sawyer—but couldn't quite make the case for pinning the murder on the number one suspect—"

"Wendell Braison," Campbell finished.

"That's correct," Gloria told him. "Wendell had his fair share of supporters, but not in this department. We went strictly by the book and believed him to be responsible for the death. We tried to get the necessary evidence to make an arrest." She frowned. "But it didn't work out, unfortunately."

That's obvious, as Dad has never gotten it out of his system, Campbell thought. "Were there any other serious suspects?" he asked, though knowing from his father and his own research into the case that no one else stood out that fit the bill.

Gloria backed this up. "No one that we could lay a finger on," she stated. "And with Wendell Braison maintaining his innocence until his death—though we had serious reservations about that—I guess that's why the case went cold over the years. Till now."

"If Braison didn't kill Lynda Boxleitner," Campbell speculated, "it means her killer could still be alive in the community—and targeted Mia O'Dell as a follow-up, for whatever reason. The different poisons used in the deaths could be strictly a matter of accessibility in different eras."

"Perhaps." Gloria planted her arms on the desk. "Or we could have *two* killers and only one still alive—and out for blood."

"True." Campbell tried to keep an open mind, though

wanting to do right by his father and believe Wendell Braison was behind the lethal poisoning of Lynda Boxleitner. If this could be proved.

"You might want to talk to Officer Jerry Napolitano," Gloria told him. "He was the first responder when Boxleitner's body was discovered and may have some thoughts. Jerry's still on the force. Unfortunately, he's currently on the Big Island of Hawaii right now, celebrating his thirty-fifth wedding anniversary with his wife, Orla."

"I'll catch up with him when he gets back," Campbell said, seeing no reason to disrupt his trip by calling. Especially since he doubted Napolitano would have much more to offer than Campbell's own father in the investigation into Lynda's death. "Thanks for your time, Chief," he said, standing.

Gloria nodded. "If O'Dell's death is in any way, shape or form associated with Boxleitner's murder, I'd love to be able to close both cases in one fell swoop. If not, getting to the root of why Mia O'Dell had to die will have to suffice. In the meantime, my door's always open."

"I'll remember that," Campbell said, knowing that his father, who had spoken highly of her as always having his back during his years on the force, felt the same way.

After leaving the office, he exchanged a few words on the investigation with Georgina, who had taken a strong interest in Mia's case. Turned out that Brandy Peñaflor, the sister of Georgina's deputy sheriff boyfriend, Ted Peñaflor, had been dealing with opioid use disorder—or opioid addiction—off and on for years. As this hit too close to home, Georgina wanted to try to get Mia's drug supplier off the streets, at the very least.

Campbell was on the same page there, though he hoped

to connect a few more points in the scheme of things that could tie together two poisonous deaths.

After leaving the building and stepping into the sunshine, he called Stefanie, wanting to invite her to dinner. He hoped she didn't have other plans.

"Hey," he said when she answered.

"Hey." Stefanie's voice had a pleasant cadence to it.

"If you're free, I was wondering if you'd like to have dinner with me this evening at my place?"

"Of course," she said quickly. "I'd be happy to join you for dinner."

"Cool." He grinned while heading toward his SUV. "Is six okay?"

"Yes, perfect."

Actually, you're perfect, Campbell thought, believing this from everything he'd come to know about her. He considered briefly asking if he could pick her up at her place but decided against this. He didn't want to make her uncomfortable in any way. "I'll text you the address."

"All right."

After he did so, Campbell climbed into his Chevy Tahoe and headed for the grocery store, en route to home, while contemplating what to cook. He imagined that Bella had already spoken to Stefanie about his visit to her estate, where—aside from talking about his latest case and Mia's checkered history as a housekeeper for Bella's father, Stuart Reston—they had shared kind words about Stefanie. She and Bella really seemed to have hit it off. Just as he had with Stefanie. He hoped that they would be able to move the needle in continuing to make progress in their relationship. So long as he didn't blow it with the dinner, Campbell was optimistic in that regard.

Chapter Ten

Admittedly, Stefanie felt downright giddy as she drove onto Campbell's property, taking note of the green, hilly acreage. She envisioned children playing and running across it merrily. Along with their doting parents watching their offspring with boundless joy.

Okay, so maybe I'm putting the cart ahead of the horse with this vision, Stefanie thought. She took a breath. Best to let things play out naturally and not assume that she and Campbell were already a match made in heaven. For now, it was just dinner—albeit a second date—and no guarantees of scrumptious desserts to leave a lasting taste in either of their mouths.

Stefanie got out of her car and approached Campbell's farmhouse. With her hair loose, she wore a sleeveless indigo denim dress and black T-strap sandals. Campbell was waiting for her when she arrived at the front door.

"Hey." He flashed her a mouthwatering grin.

"Hey." She smiled back, taking in his formfitting terracotta piqué polo shirt, beige twill chinos and brown boat shoes.

"Come in," he told her enthusiastically.

Stefanie stepped into his house and was even more impressed with the layout and rustic furnishings than she was with the land it sat on. Or at least equally so. "You have a beautiful place here," she remarked sincerely.

Campbell smiled. "Thanks. It's probably a bit much for just one person. Guess maybe I was thinking ahead—"

She grinned musingly, reading between the lines. "I see."

"Food's ready to be served," he said. "I can give you the grand tour later."

"Sounds good."

"Hope you like fish?"

Stefanie picked up the scent of the grilled halibut. "I love fish," she told him.

"Good to know." Campbell grinned. "I added tomato vinaigrette to the halibut, to go with grilled vegetables, lemon-herbed rice and whole wheat bread. There's red wine, fruit punch, water and/or coffee. Whatever suits your fancy."

She smiled. "Everything sounds tasty," she confessed. "I'll have the red wine."

"You and me both," he said flatly. "So, make yourself at home and we'll eat."

They sat kitty-corner from one another in the dining room at an aspen log table on ladder-back chairs. Stefanie had to commend Campbell for the meal. "It's really good," she marveled, which was an understatement.

"Glad you like it." He gave her a slanted grin. "Picked up a few recipes from my dad and his girlfriend, Sally. But mostly, I suppose the cooking comes naturally—if I'm motivated enough."

She giggled, slicing a knife into the grilled halibut. "I guess you were," she teased him.

"Yeah, I can certainly say unabashedly that I wanted to leave the right impression on you," he said with a laugh, then bit off a piece of bread.

Stefanie scooped up some lemon-herbed rice. "You've succeeded." She put the rice in her mouth, savoring the taste, and wondered what other tricks he might have up his sleeve.

Campbell tasted his wine. "So, I suppose Bella told you that I dropped by to talk about Mia O'Dell?"

Stefanie nodded. "I knew that Mia was the housekeeper of Bella's father," she told him. "But I didn't realize that she was stealing from Stuart Reston and was fired as a result. Not that I would've known this. Still, it kind of came as a shock. Sad, too."

"I agree on both counts," Campbell said. "Especially if losing her job was what led Mia to join the Braison Family—which may have played a crucial role in her use of fentanyl that resulted in her fatal overdose of the drug."

Stefanie's brow creased. "That would be awful, if one bad thing led to another," she stated soberly.

"Of course, whatever her own culpability was, Mia didn't deserve what she got for the bargain." Campbell stuck his fork into the grilled vegetables. "And neither did Lynda Boxleitner. The deaths occurred two decades apart—but under very similar circumstances..."

Stefanie gazed at him. "Do you still think that the two deaths are connected in some way to the Braison Family?"

Campbell sat back contemplatively, then replied with a catch to his voice, "My gut instinct says yes. But the facts, as they are currently, may tell a different story. I suppose I'll just have to keep digging till the right answers surface one way or another. In the meantime, I have someone else who's occupying my attention these days..."

Feeling the weight of his steady gaze, Stefanie couldn't

help but color as she asked playfully, "And who might that be?"

"You, Stefanie," he said clearly and concisely.

Her cheeks reddened with satisfaction. "You're occupying my attention just as much these days, Campbell," she stated candidly.

He grinned. "Good to know."

She thought this was as good a time as any to mention the gala to him. "I've been invited by Bella to the Annual Reston Hills Charitable Gala on Saturday. She's organizing it to raise money for various local causes. I'd love it if you could come as my guest..." Stefanie paused. "I know that as a police detective you probably don't have the luxury to plan anything too far ahead—"

Campbell interjected. "I'd be delighted to go to the gala as your guest, Stefanie. I'll make the time. Having been to a previous gala for guard duty, more or less, it should be fun to attend recreationally, and it's certainly a worthwhile event."

"I think so—and thanks." She showed her teeth, happy to have him accompany her to a public outing.

He echoed those thoughts, saying, "Glad to spend more time with you wherever I can."

"I feel the same," she assured him.

Before Stefanie knew it, they had leaned in to each other and started kissing. The powerful effect it had beyond her lips was instantaneous, causing her entire body to quaver.

Campbell pulled away from her swollen lips, and Stefanie, looking deeply into his eyes, asked in earnest, "Do you want to take this to your bedroom?"

"Yes." His voice was raspy. "But only if you do?"

"I want to make love to you," she responded point-blank. *How could I not, with the way you make me feel?* But she still needed to be responsible. She wasn't currently on birth control. "Do you have protection?"

"Yeah, I do," he assured her succinctly.

That was good enough for Stefanie as she rose from the table. She grabbed his arm and pulled him up toward her and uttered with anticipation, while knowing in her heart the timing was picture-perfect, "Then let's do this…"

STEFANIE WAS ANXIOUS as she stepped inside the large primary bedroom. She glanced at the hickory furniture before her eyes rested on the king-size copper-panel bed, with a dark green quilt coverlet and two large pillows. *Nice*, she thought as her gaze shifted to Campbell, who hadn't taken his own gaze off her, as though hypnotized. The notion turned her on even more.

He cupped her cheeks, and they began to kiss passionately, as Stefanie felt light on her feet. She felt the rigid contours of his body pressed against hers. Just as she had lost herself in the moment, Campbell pulled away.

"Be right back," he said on a breath.

"Okay." Stefanie watched as he went into the en suite bathroom. She started to undress, feeling strangely unabashed, while eager to see the whole of him, and to touch and be touched by him. In her heart, she knew that this was something that needed to happen—and she very much wanted it to.

When Campbell returned, he was holding a condom packet, tossing it on the bed. He peered at her and said desirously, "You're gorgeous from head to toe."

Stefanie blushed. "You think?"

"Without a single doubt," he doubled down on it, and

began removing his own clothes. They fell to the parquet floor one piece at a time as she took in his flat chest, rock-hard abs, long legs and strong feet. In between, his full manhood was clearly ready for her. As she was for him.

"I need you," Stefanie uttered, sotto voice, reaching out to him.

"I'm all yours," Campbell responded, scooping her up in his arms and carrying her to the bed.

"And I'm yours," she told him, eager to proceed on that meeting of the minds with their bodies.

Lying on the cotton sateen sheet, Stefanie waited for him to fall into her arms, half atop her, which he did. Their mouths locked for more deep kissing, and she could hear the patter of his heartbeat. Or was it her own? Either way, the craving within her was insatiable.

This only built in waves as Campbell explored her body blindly with long, nimble fingers, their lips never parting. As he stimulated her taut nipples and private parts, she nearly screamed with pleasure. Instead, she simply lay back and enjoyed it for as long as she could, before her needs went beyond that.

"Make love to me, Campbell," Stefanie demanded, stopping what he was doing, her own delight notwithstanding.

"Are you sure you're ready?" he asked selflessly.

"More than ever!" Her voice rang with determination. She went a step further, grabbing the foil packet and ripping it open. Then she took out the condom and put it on his erection, leaving no doubt as to what she wanted from him. Now.

Heeding her call, Campbell took over from there. He propped up on an elbow and calmly positioned himself between her legs. They locked eyes lasciviously as he slid slowly inside her. Stefanie adjusted her body to him and they began to make love. She planted her feet on the bed while urging him to go deeper and deeper.

As he capitulated to her wishes with abandon while fighting back his own urges, Stefanie climaxed, crying out. Her body quavered wildly as she kissed him—breathing in his enticing masculine scent—she'd nearly forgotten how good it felt to react to a man's intimate attention. She sucked in a deep breath but knew this wasn't over. Nor did she wish for it to be.

Wanting Campbell to reach his own heights of pleasure, Stefanie cooed to him, "Your turn. Let's get there together—"

"All right." Campbell sighed. He flipped her around so that he was on the bottom, and held on to Stefanie's hips firmly. She moved gradually onto him and picked up the pace as he cupped one of her buttocks and they rocked and rolled their way toward his satisfaction.

When Campbell's orgasm came, he let out a primordial grunt and his body shook. He turned them back around so Stefanie was beneath him and experienced a second climax as they soared to sexual heights like eagles in human form, in search of something rewarding that they had seized upon in their mutual pleasuring.

Afterward, both spent, they lay side by side, collecting their breaths while coming back down to earth for a safe landing. Stefanie wondered how Campbell felt, physically and mentally, now that it was over. Any regrets?

As if to alleviate any concerns on her part, Campbell laughed and said sincerely, "Wow! You were truly amazing."

Coloring, Stefanie breathed a sigh of relief. "So were you."

"Some things in life are worth waiting for. This definitely qualifies."

She chuckled. "I'd have to agree with you there. It was certainly a good thing to wait for this to happen—and then achieve the desired results."

"Amen to that." Campbell laughed, then kissed her shoulder. "Next time, though—now that the sense of urgency was met—I'd like to take it nice and slow so that we prolong the intimacy as long as we can while enjoying the pleasures of sex."

"Mmm..." Stefanie tingled inside at the notion, that there would be a next time. "You'll get no argument from me there."

"Good." He kissed the top of her head. "I hate arguing, especially where it concerns matters of the heart."

"Me, too." She liked hearing him think of sexual relations between them as relating to the rhythm of their hearts.

Stefanie also wanted to see this as the start—or continuation—of something special that had lots of upside for the future. Maybe it was truly their destiny to meet the way they met, to lead to what just happened and could happen beyond. Campbell took her into his arms, and she fell asleep on that sweet thought.

As he got up the next morning, Campbell could not deny that Stefanie had more than measured up to any fantasies he'd had about going to bed with her. Beyond the hot sex, the chemistry between them in general was undeniable. The fact that the two of them both seemed to be on the same page—now that they had gotten that first night of intimate relations out of their system—in forging ahead, gave him hope that he might finally have found someone that pushed the right buttons in what he wanted from a partner for the long term.

Stefanie had done just that in no time flat. Campbell watched as she was still sound asleep—lying on her stomach beneath the coverlet, her face pressed sideways against the pillow while looking absolutely beautiful—no doubt needing some rest after their sexual escapades had worked their way into a second round that was even more frenetic and all-consuming than the first.

He was still in reverie mode when Stefanie opened her eyes. Yawning attractively, she looked at him and asked, "How long have you been awake?"

Campbell grinned and responded, "Just long enough to be able to appreciate how hot you look sleeping in my bed."

Stefanie blushed. "You would say that."

"I only tell it like it is," he said truthfully, knowing that she was checking him out as well, still in the nude. "I was about to hop into the shower. If you need a little more shut-eye, I can wake you afterwards and make us breakfast."

"I'm good," she said, rubbing her eyes. "Why don't I join you in the shower and then we'll have breakfast?"

"Okay." He smiled, picturing them fooling around in the shower while putting the soap bar to good use. This turned him on. As did much about her. Even while in the back of his mind duty still called, as he tried to solve at least one case of a fatal OD under mysterious circumstances. Which may or may not be associated with a similar incident that occurred way before his time.

Chapter Eleven

Campbell pulled into Chao's Auto Repair on Sixteenth Street. He was hoping to find Irving Quinaz, a thirty-two-year-old auto mechanic with a criminal record that involved drug dealing. According to a bartender at the Kieke's Nightclub on Lour Avenue, Mia O'Dell was identified as having been there on the Saturday night before Founder's Day and leaving with Quinaz. The location itself was pinpointed as a result of cell phone data that revealed Mia's cell phone—which was still missing—had pinged close to the nightclub a short time prior to her estimated time of death.

It was the last time the phone was on to record her location before it went dead. Considering the timeline and circumstances, Campbell definitely suspected Quinaz was a person of interest in supplying Mia with the fentanyl mixed with carfentanil that killed her. If this was the case, was it an unintentional lethal dose? Or did he willfully kill her—perhaps at the behest of someone else? Such as Kenneth Braison?

Stepping into the auto shop garage, Campbell spotted—working under the hood of a Buick Enclave—a man who fit the description of Irving Quinaz's mug shot. When he looked up, Campbell saw that he had brown eyes and brown hair in a high fade style, was of medium build and about six feet tall.

He regarded Campbell and asked nonchalantly, "Can I help you?"

"Are you Irving Quinaz?"

"Yeah, who are you?"

Flashing his identification, Campbell replied coolly, "Detective Sawyer, Reston Hills PD. I'd like to ask you a few questions about Mia O'Dell—"

Quinaz jutted his chin. "What about her?"

So, he's not denying that he knows Mia, Campbell told himself, stepping closer to the suspect. "She died on Founder's Day from a drug overdose. Do you happen to know anything about that" —Campbell watched his uneasy reaction— "as the man identified seen leaving the Kieke's Nightclub with Mia on Saturday, the night before she wound up naked and dead in Reston Hills Park?"

Quinaz knitted thick brows. "Look, I heard about that, but I had nothing to do with it, okay? We met at the club, hooked up in the back of my Toyota Highlander and went our separate ways. Never saw her again. End of story—"

Campbell peered at him. Even if plausible, he wasn't quite ready to leave it at that. "Did you provide Mia with fentanyl during this hook up?"

"No—definitely not!" Quinaz insisted.

"You have a record that suggests otherwise," Campbell put forth.

"I was a kid when I got involved with the wrong people at the wrong time in the drug culture." Quinaz blew out a loud breath. "I did no time and have kept my nose clean ever since. Wherever Mia got the fentanyl, it didn't come from me."

Campbell mulled that over. He had always believed in second chances—for both mistakes made and romance. Maybe Quinaz deserved the benefit of the doubt. Or not.

"Did Mia ever mention anything to you about the Braison Family?"

Quinaz met his eyes. "Yeah, she said she was a member but might be getting out of the cult."

"Did she say why?"

"Only that it wasn't everything it was cracked up to be...and that something better was maybe about to come her way." He scratched his head. "She didn't say what that was. And I never asked."

Campbell couldn't help but wonder what that was all about. Was that the fentanyl-carfentanil combo creating an unrealistic fantasy in Mia's head before she OD'd on it? Or could she have found herself a sugar daddy outside the cult—who maybe she tried to blackmail and then paid the ultimate price?

Or was Kenneth Braison determined to keep her in the fold, whatever it took? Even if it meant making an example out of her in wanting to break free of his hold as a cult leader.

Campbell cast his eyes on the mechanic and asked him straightforwardly, "What time did this hookup between you and Mia end?"

"Around midnight," Quinaz answered with no runup.

"Hmm. And what did you do after that?"

"I drove home," he insisted.

"What about Mia?" Campbell asked, noting that the nightclub was less than a mile from Reston Hills Park. "Did you see her with anyone else?"

Quinaz shook his head. "She just walked off." He

paused. "Thought about asking if she wanted a lift. But I had the feeling—don't ask me why—that she either already had a ride or had other plans that didn't involve me…"

"Okay." Campbell wasn't necessarily sold on his story but couldn't dispute it as yet. He considered the possibility that Mia had gotten a ride with either a known or unknown person. Or may have walked to the park and could have been followed there. Or someone was waiting for her at the park, or she encountered them randomly—and was handed the lethal drug combo.

Maybe surveillance cameras can give us something, Campbell thought. He looked Quinaz in the eye and said warningly, "If I have any further questions, I'll be back."

"Fine by me," Quinaz said with a shrug. "I'm not going anywhere."

Campbell walked out of the garage, believing that it was likely a dead end with the mechanic, while providing more food for thought otherwise. He got in his SUV and drove off, wondering if Mia could have somehow gotten in over her head through one means or another. Over and beyond her exposure to fentanyl.

JASMINE WASN'T QUITE sure who to trust as she walked around the compound, trying to avoid eye contact with anyone who might become suspicious of her and report this to Kenneth or Juan. She did her best to appear as unbothered as possible when it came to Mia being dead from a drug overdose. After all, it seemed as though most of the Braison Family members had come to terms with her death, as if it was just something that happened and not their concern.

But Jasmine saw it differently. She didn't believe that Mia would knowingly ingest fentanyl, putting her life on the line. Not to mention disappointing Kenneth—if, in fact, he wasn't the one who'd handed her the fentanyl in the first place. At least on the surface, he appeared adamantly against drug use on the property.

Yet beneath the surface, Jasmine feared that the Braison Family was pretty much capable of anything. Even murder, if anyone dared to challenge Kenneth's authority. While making it appear to be a self-inflicted overdose.

Was this what had happened to Mia—who could be headstrong and independent-minded, unlike most of the followers? Had she been murdered to keep her silenced forever? Had she learned secrets that made her a liability?

Jasmine sucked in a deep breath as she forced a smile at this follower and that one, but kept her mouth shut. Why hadn't Kenneth been more forthcoming when she expressed her concerns to him about Mia and her totally unexpected and premature death? Why did he, instead, blow her off and go through the same old Braison Family principles as a way to avoid the subject?

Did someone in the Family have it in for Mia—with or without Kenneth's knowledge or consent—and coax her into OD'ing and being left naked and humiliated at the park?

Jasmine wondered if Stefanie might be able to provide her with any answers, if only for her own peace of mind. And to help her decide if she wanted to remain a member of the Braison Family. She and Stefanie had exchanged phone numbers, with Stefanie encouraging her to call if she ever needed to talk—almost as though this was expected of her.

I'll do it—give her a call and maybe we can meet up somewhere away from prying eyes and talk, Jasmine told herself. She glanced over her shoulder as if someone were watching her. While no one stood out, she spotted Siobhan, who tried to pretend she was too busy on her cell phone to notice her—but never seemed to miss a beat when being on the lookout for anything she could report back to Kenneth or Juan. Jasmine couldn't help but wonder if Mia had felt the same way. Before disaster struck like a tornado.

IN HER LIVING ROOM, Stefanie sat on the copper-colored MCM chair, watching television. Or at least she was trying to, gazing at the fifty-five-inch smart TV on the wall. It was hard to concentrate with Curlie on her lap trying to decide whether to be still or spry, per her cat nature.

Beyond that, Stefanie couldn't help but think about her night of passion with Campbell, awakening desires in her she never knew she had. The way he reacted to her touch, kisses and more, she believed that he, too, was feeling it. So yes, she believed that they had started dating officially, more or less. This scared her as much as exhilarated her, as venturing into new territory in a Reston Hills relationship with sex as a part of the equation meant moving into the next phase of starting over as a widow.

Was she really up for this? Would Campbell protect her heart as she needed in forging ahead and making the most of the opportunity that they had both been afforded?

And would she be able to give him everything he needed in a woman, lover and friend as he traded in his single status for becoming boyfriend material?

Stefanie looked even further ahead at the prospects

of matrimony, children, meeting Campbell's dad and his partner—and how this all might play out—if she and Campbell remained serious about each other over the long haul.

There you go overthinking things again, Stefanie admonished herself. She would not go there. *Just let things happen as they're meant to—or not*, she thought, enjoying the ride in the meantime.

Curlie grew restless and jumped from her lap onto the floor, where the cat then ran off to be by herself. Stefanie chuckled with amusement, then turned back to the TV screen to focus on the old romance movie she was trying to watch.

When her cell phone rang a few minutes later, Stefanie removed it from the pocket of her denim shorts and saw that the caller was Jasmine, from the Braison Family. Answering the call, masking her surprise, in spite of having invited Jasmine to do just that in getting more info from her on Mia, Stefanie said cheerily, "Hi, Jasmine."

"Can we meet…to talk?" Jasmine asked, sounding tense.

"Of course." Stefanie pressed the phone closer to her ear. "Where?"

"How about Reston Hills Park?"

"That's fine," Stefanie agreed.

Jasmine said, ill at ease, "I'll wait for you near the south entry to the river walk…"

Before Stefanie could say anything else, the phone had disconnected.

NEEDLESS TO SAY, Stefanie's interest was piqued as she drove to the park. Had Jasmine learned something about

Mia's death that she needed to get off her chest? Something that Jasmine wasn't at liberty to say at the Braison Family compound under the auspices of Kenneth Braison?

After reaching Reston Hills Park, which brought back unsettling memories from Founder's Day, Stefanie parked in a lot on the south side and went to look for Jasmine.

She found her quickly enough, as Jasmine came out of the woods, wearing the shoulder tote Stefanie remembered from when they first met.

Jasmine said in an uneven tone, "Thanks for coming," and gave her a hug as if they were old friends.

"Sure." Stefanie offered her a disconcerting look. "What is it?"

Jasmine looked over her shoulder, as if expecting someone to come and attack them at any moment, before eyeing her warily and responding, "Let's move away from here..."

Stefanie nodded. "All right."

They made their way onto the tree-lined walkway on the banks of the Beeks River and ambled along.

After a long moment or two, Jasmine faced Stefanie and batting her eyes, said expressively, "You were the one who discovered Mia's body in the park on Founder's Day?"

"Yes," Stefanie acknowledged. "It was shortly after you handed me the flyer that day. I was actually hoping to talk to you about that when I visited the Braison Family ranch. But then Kenneth and Juan kept that from happening..."

"I know." Jasmine nodded, wrinkling her nose. "I was shocked to hear about Mia's death—and especially the way she died..."

"Are you saying she wasn't using drugs...fentanyl?" Stefanie asked.

"Not to my knowledge." Jasmine wrung her hands nervously. "That's what is so weird about this. Why would Mia OD on fentanyl...unless she was unaware it had entered her system?"

The same thought had crossed Stefanie's mind more than once. She regarded Jasmine and asked, "So, you think someone—maybe from inside the Braison Family—gave the drug to her deliberately? And if so, for what reason?"

Jasmine chewed on her lower lip. "I've asked myself that," she muttered. "All I can think of is that Mia may have found out something that put her at odds with the Family. Especially if she threatened to expose publicly whatever she knew. Kenneth would never have allowed that to happen—"

Stefanie swallowed thickly and asked, "To the point of killing her to keep Mia's silence?"

"Honestly, I wouldn't put it past him," she said uneasily. "Kenneth would do anything to protect whatever secrets he had. Or could otherwise ruin what he and his father, Wendell Braison, had built over decades." Jasmine drew a sigh. "I just don't know..."

"Have you spoken to anyone in the Family about this?" Stefanie wondered.

"I tried talking to Kenneth, but he just dismissed my concerns as if they had no merit whatsoever. I wasn't about to speak with any other members of the Braison Family, only to potentially put myself at risk..." She looked behind them and back at Stefanie with frightened eyes. "Even now, I'm taking a big risk in talking to you about this…"

"You know, you don't have to go back to the compound," Stefanie stressed to her. "If you feel your life is in danger—"

"I do…but I don't," Jasmine told her. "They think that I'm here passing out more flyers—" she lifted a few out of her tote bag to illustrate and then put them back in it "—in trying to recruit new followers. Which is why I need to get back, before they start asking questions…" She sighed. "Most of Kenneth's followers are there for the right reasons. That includes me. I don't want to mess things up for them by airing my suspicions to the authorities…" She paused, then admitted, "I did try to talk to Detective Sawyer when the police searched the compound, but was unable to do so without being seen by others."

Stefanie gazed at her. "I can certainly speak with Detective Sawyer, if you like," she volunteered.

"Would you?"

"Yes. But without any hard proof to support your suspicions—and mine, frankly—I'm not sure he will be able to do much in terms of putting pressure on Kenneth and the Braison Family."

"Too bad." Jasmine furrowed her brow. "Kenneth knows how to cover his tracks well, so I guess we're stuck."

"Not necessarily," Stefanie argued as they continued to walk. "The police investigation into Mia's death is still ongoing. Don't underestimate their ability to get to the truth—one way or another…"

Jasmine nodded. "Hope so. For Mia. She wasn't

perfect—who is?—but she really did want to make the world a better place in her own way. Just as I do."

"Don't we all," Stefanie said idealistically. Unfortunately, the world would always be a dangerous place for some more than others. But that didn't mean there was any harm in maintaining a positive attitude, at the very least. Even if being in a cult was not the way for her to go. And apparently was a wrong choice for Mia, too.

Jasmine said warily, "Anyway, I have to go."

"All right." Stefanie touched her arm. "Please be careful—and don't try to do anything that will put you at risk…"

Jasmine nodded. "I won't," she promised and took Stefanie's hands. "Pray for Mia's soul, as I will."

Stefanie agreed to this, then watched as Jasmine scurried off, disappearing into the woods.

Chapter Twelve

On Saturday evening, the Annual Reston Hills Charitable Gala, held at the Menakerr Center on Sallis Way in downtown Reston Hills, was in full swing. A five-member band was onstage performing live upbeat music, with author book readings, performances by talented children, an auction to raise money for local programs and enough interesting food choices to go around.

Stefanie felt slightly out of her element as she stood in the auction room, wearing a lilac cap-sleeve gown with strap sandals. Her hair was in chignon. Standing on one side of her was Campbell, who was resplendent in a crisp gray suit and tie over a baby blue shirt, worn with black oxfords. On the other side was Bella, who was stunning as always, in a sleek, black one-shoulder ponté knit gown and matching pointed-toe pumps. Next to her was Bella's date for the gala, Russell Kercheval, a fortysomething pro golfer, who was tall and slender, with wavy salt-and-pepper hair in a side-swept style. He wore a black tuxedo and black derby shoes. According to Bella, it wasn't serious.

Stefanie took her word for that, knowing that Bella seemed content at the moment to play the field while putting her efforts into being the perfect ambassador for Reston Hills.

Bella, one arm tucked beneath Russell's, flashed her teeth at Stefanie and Campbell, and asked, "Hope you're having fun?"

"Absolutely," Campbell said in an upbeat voice, holding a flute of champagne.

"I feel the same," Stefanie assured her, wanting the gala to be a big success.

"Me too." Russell grinned and kissed Bella on the cheek. "Always fun to be in your company, Bella."

"Then we're all in agreement." Bella laughed, seeming to soak in the compliment. "Now, let's see if the auction can bring in some big bucks for the right programs and causes…"

"I'm happy to do my part," Stefanie told her, "with my donation of free yoga and tai chi lessons for two winning bidders, respectively."

Campbell pitched in, "As am I, having offered a free trail ride for two at my father's horse ranch in nearby Fallon's Creek."

"They're great donations!" Bella's face lit up. "And should fetch some nice bids."

"As should the free golf lessons that I was happy to donate," Russell said, as if not wanting to be outdone.

"Another winning ticket for would-be golfers," Bella exclaimed. "Thank you, Russ."

He beamed. "Anytime."

After Bella made her way to the podium, with Russell close behind, Campbell commented, "She really is made for these civic duties and keeping her great-grandfather's town alive and well, with a bright future."

"True." Stefanie smiled and sipped her champagne. She couldn't help but wonder if their own future had brightness written all over it. They seemed to be headed in the right direction, giving her reason for being optimistic.

She wished she felt the same way about Jasmine Roxburgh. If it were up to Stefanie, she would just as soon see Jasmine leave the Braison Family. But clearly this was something that she was reluctant to do, as if Kenneth and company had a hold on her that Jasmine couldn't break free of.

I can only hope that she protects herself from harm, even if that means getting out of there, Stefanie thought. She wondered if this was what had proved to be Mia's downfall—being unable to escape danger. Even if it was staring her right in the face. Till it was too late to prevent her own death.

Campbell got her attention when he asked Stefanie, "I heard music coming from the ballroom. Can I have this dance?"

Stefanie didn't necessarily consider dancing to be her strong suit, but with Campbell she felt she was up for just about anything. So, she responded readily, "Of course. Let's go dance…"

CAMPBELL WAS ONLY too happy to get Stefanie on the dance floor to a nice slow and sensual torch song the band was playing. It gave them an opportunity to show off as one of the newest couples in Reston Hills—competing, he suspected, for that honor with Bella and Russell, who seemed really into each other. Campbell wasn't at all surprised to see that dancing with Stefanie, her head resting comfortably on his shoulder, seemed entirely natural and she felt damned good in his arms in a public setting.

To say nothing of how wonderful she felt in a private setting, where only they could see what one another brought to the table in terms of affection and intimacy. He could only imagine how much more they had to offer to each other, while reaping the benefits left and right. North and south. East and west.

"You're pretty good at this," Stefanie told him, bringing Campbell back into focus with the moment at hand and the gala, which looked to be an enormous success for the community.

He held her a little closer as they danced, and replied, "I could say the same for you. Guess that means that we make one hell of a couple on the dance floor."

"That, we do." She laughed. "And not so bad off the floor as well."

Campbell chuckled, in total agreement. He kissed Stefanie, tasting the champagne off her mouth. "You've got that right." Honestly, he could dance the night away with her every night—given the way their bodies molded together in total harmony—were there not other things both had on their plates.

As it was, for him, there remained the Mia O'Dell case to solve. There was still a question as to who supplied her the fentanyl-carfentanil concoction. And whether or not it was for nefarious reasons, over and beyond the illegality associated with drug dealing that resulted in a death. Until these things could be answered, there would be no rest for the weary as far as the case was concerned.

Along with that, Campbell still could not shake the feeling that Mia's death was connected in some meaningful way with the death of Lynda Boxleitner—apart from, or perhaps in conjunction with, both women being members of the Braison Family. Or maybe he was reading this wrong and only wanted that to be true as a way to clear up both his case and the cold case his father left behind.

When the song ended—too soon, as far as Campbell was concerned—Stefanie suggested they head back to the auction to see if Bella presented anything that might be worth bidding on for them.

"I'm game for that," Campbell responded.

Stefanie smiled. "Good. Maybe later, we can get in another dance or whatever you'd like to do."

"Sounds good," he said wistfully, taking her hand as they headed out of the ballroom.

THAT NIGHT, THEY went back to Stefanie's house and wasted little time before ending up in her bedroom. Campbell took one look around at the attractive MCM furniture, then zeroed in on the bamboo-platform queen-size bed with an aquamarine comforter. Picturing Stefanie beneath it, naked and ready, got him aroused.

"So, what's next?" he teased her after pulling her close to him.

"Um…" Her lashes batted flirtatiously. "Any suggestions…?"

"Yeah, I have one." Campbell cupped her cheeks and kissed her lips. He loved the softness of them.

"Just one?" she uttered into his mouth.

He grinned desirously. "For starters."

They kissed again. Minutes later, hot and bothered, they were in bed and deep into foreplay. After Campbell slipped on protection, mutual stimulation slowly but surely turned into lovemaking, where each gave as much—if not more—than they received, stretching well into the night.

Running his hands through Stefanie's long hair while they made love was a turn-on for Campbell all on its own. As well as hearing her cry out when an orgasm caused her body to respond spasmodically. His climax came shortly after and was equally intense, his breathing heightened during the peak moment of satisfaction.

Stefanie giggled from atop him. "You're insatiable. Or maybe I'm the guilty party here."

Campbell laughed, enjoying the weight of her against his body. "I think we're both into each other enough to make a full confession," he said jokingly.

"I agree." She leaned over and gave him a long kiss, before rolling off him.

While they lay there catching their breath and allowing their heart rates to get back to normal, all Campbell could think of was that this was something he never wanted to see end. But it went beyond that. He was starting to feel something akin to love, even if it still needed a bit more time being spent together. But his gut instinct told him that Stefanie was a special woman who was roping him in like one of his dad's quarter horses. And he didn't mind her being at the reins one bit.

ON SUNDAY MORNING, Stefanie sat with Campbell at the Notton Street Café. They were waiting for Jasmine, who Stefanie had managed to talk into slipping away from the Braison Family ranch and speaking with Campbell about her suspicions surrounding Mia's death.

Maybe nothing will come out of it, Stefanie told herself

as she drank her coffee. But at least Campbell was open to an informal chat with Jasmine—the one person from the cult who seemed willing to speak her mind about its inner workings and how this may have played a pivotal role in Mia's lethal overdose—considering that Jasmine was panicked at the thought of meeting with Campbell for an official interview.

Stefanie thought, *Can I really blame her?* After Mia's death and the hold Kenneth Braison seemed to have over his followers, challenging his authority was a risky venture at best. And could prove to be a fatal move at worst.

Fortunately, Campbell took this into consideration as he welcomed an insider's perspective on what she knew and didn't know about the Braison Family. And Kenneth, in particular.

For her part, Stefanie felt an obligation to bring the two together, since Jasmine had reached out to her for help. At least it felt that way when reading between the lines, irregular as they may have been.

Stefanie sipped more coffee as she gazed at Campbell and thought about their latest night of passion and what it meant in moving ahead in their relationship. She was all in with him in seeing where this went. He had made her believe that he felt the same way and wanted this to work out, well beyond the red-hot sex between them. This gave her confidence that their journey had only just begun, with lots of blue skies and symmetry ahead for them.

Campbell met her eyes and grinned. "You're gorgeous," he stated once again, as though he couldn't help himself.

Stefanie blushed. "I never tire of hearing that," she had to admit.

"Good, because I intend to keep reminding you of one of the many great elements that has me hooked."

"Umm..." She gave a soft smile, allowing that to sink in graciously.

Clutching his coffee mug, Campbell said, thoughtful, "So, do you think Jasmine is coming? Or was she prevented from doing so by the Braison Family?"

Stefanie suspected that the second question was more rhetorical in nature, even if a legitimate concern. "I know she wants to talk to you, even if she's afraid to do so. I can call her, if you want..."

Before he could respond, Campbell's own cell phone rang. He removed it from the side pocket of his blazer, glanced at it and said, "I better get this—"

Stefanie nodded and looked on as he listened to and spoke with someone from the police department. He exchanged a few more words as a distressed expression spread across this face, then told the person he was on his way and disconnected.

"What is it?" Stefanie asked, peering at him.

"Some disturbing news..." Campbell sucked in a deep breath and answered soberly, "An African American female's body has been found in Reston Hills Park." He ran a hand across his mouth. "The dead woman has tentatively been identified as Braison Family member Jasmine Roxburgh..."

Stefanie's jaw dropped as the gravity of what she'd just heard weighed on her. Jasmine dead? How? Had someone from the Braison Family come after her to prevent her from talking to Campbell? Or was there another reason why she, like Mia, was now dead?

CAMPBELL WOULD HAVE preferred to take Stefanie back to her house en route to the crime scene. But, as he expected, she would have none of it—insisting on accompanying him to the park. She had blamed herself prematurely for Jasmine's death. He had strongly pushed back against that, certain that whatever the cause—especially if criminal in intent—the onus would lie on entirely whoever was responsible. Stefanie had acquiesced to this, more or less, even as Campbell contemplated the latest casualty to befall a member of the Braison Family.

He glanced at Stefanie in the passenger seat and warned nevertheless, "Let's not jump to any conclusions."

She blinked. "If you mean beyond the fact that Jasmine's dead, I'll try not to."

"All right." Campbell felt that was the best he could hope for, for the time being. He turned back to the windshield, wondering if it had been wise to agree to meet with Jasmine clandestinely rather than in a police interview room. But since she had already spoken with Stefanie and might have had something useful to offer in the investigation into Mia O'Dell's death, it seemed like good idea. Particularly when Mia was reluctant to go on record officially with potential repercussions from the Braison Family. Campbell could only wonder if Jasmine had found herself caught in such a trap with no way out.

When they arrived at Reston Hills Park and got close to the area where the body was discovered, Detective Georgina Alvarez was waiting there to greet them.

"Hey," she said flatly, having been the one to identify Jasmine after discovering a tote bag with her driver's license near the scene where her body was found.

"Hey." Campbell introduced Georgina to Stefanie and

vice versa, knowing that the detective was aware of their ongoing personal relationship. "Stefanie and Jasmine were friends," he said, to explain Stefanie's presence at a potential crime scene. "We were supposed to meet with Jasmine at a diner this morning to address her concerns about the Braison Family and Mia O'Dell's drug overdose." He frowned. "But she never showed up..."

"I doubt she ever had a chance to." Georgina sighed heavily. "Judging by her body—which was discovered by a woman who was walking her Finnish Lapphund dog—I'm guessing that Jasmine's been dead for at least a few hours."

Stefanie's brow creased. "How?"

"That'll be up to the coroner to determine," Georgina replied.

Campbell nodded and cast his eyes at Stefanie. "You'll need to wait here." Aside from it being a possible crime scene that didn't need to be disturbed, he saw no need to subject her to having to witness firsthand—up close and personal—another dead body.

Stefanie gave him an understanding look. "All right," she uttered meekly.

He moved away from her, alongside Georgina, and headed toward the decedent, who was lying near a trail on the other side of the park from where Mia was discovered.

"There she is..." Georgina muttered.

Campbell trained his eyes on the nude body of Jasmine Roxburgh. She was lying on her side on the grass in a fetal position—almost looking like she was taking a nap, with part of her blond Afro acting as a pillow. Her toenails had green polish on them. There were no outward signs of trauma. He noted the initials KB tattooed onto her right forearm, as if to remind him that Jasmine was a certified follower of Kenneth Braison—which may have cost Jasmine her life.

Campbell remarked instinctively, "I suspect that Jasmine, like Mia O'Dell, OD'd on fentanyl and carfentanil."

Georgina nodded. "I was thinking the same thing. Once the coroner's office confirms this, the next question is, where did she get the drug or drugs, and was she a victim of drug abuse—or deliberately murdered?"

"Yeah." Campbell gazed again at the attractive young woman whose voice had been forever silenced for one reason or another. "It's not a stretch to believe that however this plays out, Jasmine's death is tied to Mia's and their involvement with the Braison Family." *And, by extension, the murder of Lynda Boxleitner*, he told himself, sensing that the parallels could not be rejected out of hand. Even when the proof had yet to be established.

"I'm in agreement with you there," Georgina said firmly. "We just need to get the goods on Kenneth Braison or his cohorts to make the case."

Campbell jutted his chin. "If it's there, we'll uncover it…" He turned to where Stefanie was still standing—anxious, no doubt. "I need to go fill her in."

"Do it." Georgina nodded. She put a hand on his shoulder. "Sorry she's being put through this—again…"

"Me too." Campbell wished that weren't the case, but it was the hand both he and Stefanie had been dealt. Now they needed to see it through—for better, hopefully, or worse.

Chapter Thirteen

The area where Stefanie had been forced to remain while Campbell went to view the body had been cordoned off by police. She could only lament at the thought that Jasmine had died all of a sudden, if true. The same day they were supposed to meet up with Jasmine to talk about her concerns regarding Kenneth Braison and his cult possibly being complicit in Mia's death, Jasmine had been found dead, too?

What gives? Stefanie asked herself, pacing as she awaited Campbell's return. *This is getting too weird.* How could this happen? Could the two deaths be entirely coincidental and therefore unrelated? Or were they definitely related?

And could they be tied to a cold case homicide that Campbell's father had investigated?

As Stefanie pondered these questions, she took a breath and looked up to find Campbell standing there, gazing at her, having come across the barricade tape.

"Hey," he said in a low voice.

She met his eyes and asked, "What did you find out?"

Campbell hesitated, rubbing his jawline. "Jasmine appears to have died under similar circumstances to Mia...

right down to having her clothes removed. The autopsy will show if she OD'd on fentanyl or another lethal drug."

Stefanie put a hand to her mouth as she envisioned Jasmine lying there and then switched the ghastly image to Mia. "In talking to Jasmine, I didn't get the impression that she was a drug user."

"Maybe she wasn't," he entertained.

"So, we're talking about murder?"

Campbell lowered his chin. "We'll see about that," he responded ruminatively. "Don't want to get ahead of myself by speculating. But clearly, Jasmine's mysterious death—coming when and how it did—is cause for concern."

For me, too, Stefanie told herself, putting it mildly. She said, ill at ease, "The Braison Family has a lot of explaining to do. Or will Kenneth Braison try to worm his way out of this death of one of his followers, too…?"

"If Braison or his Family are culpable in any way for Jasmine's death—or Mia's, for that matter—they'll have to answer for it, one way or another," Campbell promised, leaving it at that. He put a gentle arm around her shoulders. "I'll take you home."

Though she wanted to stick with him every step of the way in the investigation, Stefanie understood that she needed to stay in her own lane and allow him to do the police work. All she could do was hope he could get the right answers on why Mia and now Jasmine were dead seemingly without legitimate reasons.

CAMPBELL FLASHED HIS ID as he stood at the gate to the Braison Family compound, under the watchful eyes of

Juan Barrientos and a hefty, bald guard, over six feet tall with a moon-shaped scar on his cheek.

"I need to see Braison!" Campbell said sharply.

Juan smirked. "Uh, Kenneth's kind of busy right now. What is this all about?" he demanded.

"You'll know when you know," Campbell retorted, glancing at the other man, preferring not to give Braison a heads-up on the nature of the visit.

Juan seemed to think about offering resistance, but thought better of it as he got out a cell phone from the back pocket of his jeans and put it to his ear. "There's a detective here to see you…" Campbell watched him listen expressionlessly, then Juan hung up and muttered, "Follow me…"

They left the other man standing guard, and Campbell was led to one of the cabins. Kenneth stepped out of it with two attractive and slender young blond-haired women, who grinned at him coquettishly, then scattered as the cult leader approached them.

Kenneth peered at Campbell and said snidely, "This is becoming rather habit forming. To what do I owe this pleasure, Detective Sawyer, *this* time around?"

Meeting his hard gaze, Campbell answered succinctly, "Another one of your followers, Jasmine Roxburgh, was found dead this morning in Reston Hills Park—"

Kenneth's countenance changed. "What?"

"She was naked and, apparently, left there to die…" Campbell faced Juan, who seemed impassive, then turned back to the cult leader. "An autopsy will show if there were any drugs in Jasmine's system that may have contributed to her death. Or any other explanation for what happened to her—"

After sucking in a deep breath, Kenneth stated somberly, "I'm frankly stunned to hear about Jasmine's death. She was a valued member of the Braison Family...as was Mia..."

"Now both women are dead," Campbell said, an edge to his voice. "And under circumstances that I would call highly suspicious."

"Believe me, I feel the same way," Kenneth argued. "So does Juan. We're family, and what hurts one of us, hurts us all. I wish I could tell you why either of them had to die, but I can't. I can only say that Jasmine, like Mia and every other member of the Family, are free to go outside the compound whenever the spirit moves them. In fact, we encourage members to step into the real world and its many problems as often as they like—so that they can better appreciate what we offer to the contrary in what I see as a much better world within this space we've created here." He scratched his circle beard. "I fear that both Jasmine and Mia were influenced by those on the dark side, and it took them down a very dark path of no return—resulting in drug abuse and suicidal behavior."

Braison's almost too smooth an operator, Campbell thought. Only he wasn't buying it. At least not the notion that the two deaths had nothing to do with the Braison Family and everything to do with the outside world and its negative influences. As far as Campbell was concerned, all roads in this investigation still led back to the cult's compound. In one respect or another.

He narrowed his eyes at the two men and said, "Once the estimated time of death is established, I'll need to know where you both were—and, for that matter, every member of your Family."

"Not a problem," Kenneth said. "Nothing to hide. Neither of us have stepped outside the compound for the last twenty-four hours, at least."

"That's right," Juan backed him up. "We've been swamped with one thing after another in trying to keep things running smoothly. Anyone can vouch for that."

"Anyone but Jasmine Roxburgh and Mia O'Dell." Campbell rolled his eyes. "They somehow seemed to have slipped out unnoticed—and apparently, with little concern about their health and well-being away from this ranch—while ending up naked and dead in the park all by themselves. Doesn't really sound like a close-knit family who have each other's backs to me when the going gets tough—as in death."

Kenneth furrowed his brow and spat out, "You don't know what you're talking about—any more than your father did when he tried to railroad my father by looking for darkness—but only finding the light within the Braison Family orbit. We're not the enemy, Detective, no matter how much you want to make us out to be this radical group of misfits and weirdos. Now, unless you're here to arrest me, I suggest you be on your way and track down whoever is responsible for either Jasmine's or Mia's deaths—if they weren't self-inflicted. You won't find the person on this ranch…"

That's still open for debate, Campbell told himself, in spite of the cult leader's words to the contrary. It stung to insinuate that his dad was out to get Wendell Braison without just cause. As it did to imply that Braison's son was merely the misunderstood victim of a witch hunt. Or warlock.

All things considered, Campbell preferred to believe

that there was something to the Braison Family involvement in the mysterious deaths of three women spanning two decades. He intended to keep up the pressure on Kenneth Braison and his cult to find answers—till he was satisfied that they were barking up the wrong tree.

Campbell shot him a cold stare and said curtly, "If you have nothing to hide, then you have nothing to worry about with this investigation. But if the evidence indicates otherwise, then you've got a real problem that this compound won't protect you from." He took a breath and added thoughtfully, "And just for the record, as a police detective, my father was only doing his job—going wherever the case led him. The fact that it was never solved doesn't mean he wasn't on the right track. Or that the same track has come full circle in bridging the past with the present investigation…"

Campbell left it at that and walked away from the two men, wondering if he would be any more successful in establishing a clear link to the Braison Family in Jasmine's and Mia's deaths than his dad had been in making the case in linking Wendell Braison to Lynda Boxleitner's murder.

KENNETH WAS FROWNING as he observed Campbell Sawyer exit the Braison Family property, a swagger to the detective's step. It was bad enough that another one of his followers, Jasmine, had died so soon after Mia's death—and apparently under similar circumstances. Worse, though, was that it put the Family—and him, in particular—under the microscope. Much like when his father was at the helm two decades ago and became the target of an investigation that went nowhere—but his father had never quite been able to get out from beneath the specter of being an alleged murderer.

This didn't set well with Kenneth. Whether or not his father, Wendell Braison, had actually poisoned to death Lynda Boxleitner—one of his many bedmates—and gotten away with it was irrelevant in present day terms. Wasn't it? His father, whatever his faults, deserved to rest in peace, just like his mother did.

But Kenneth wondered about his own peace of mind while still among the living. Would the detective continue to hound him, hoping to pin two deaths on him while tarnishing the intent and reputation of the Braison Family? Or would the investigation veer off in a different direction and Campbell, along with the meddlesome yoga instructor he was bedding, Stefanie Nguyen, leave well enough alone? So they could finally go about their business and mission as a family without further interference.

Juan interrupted his thoughts by asking scornfully, "So, do you think the detective is going to lay off us?"

"Only when he has good reason to look elsewhere," Kenneth answered truthfully, rolling his long fingers through this hair. "But he doesn't have nearly enough smoke to start a fire. Otherwise, Campbell would be making arrests. He's got nothing..." Or at least not enough substance that Kenneth felt would ultimately hit the mark.

"Yeah, I'm thinking the same thing," Juan muttered, scratching his head. "They're looking for scapegoats within the Family—instead of going after outsiders who hate us and must have targeted Jasmine and Mia to make examples out of us."

"Perhaps..." Kenneth set his jaw. "Gather everyone to meet in front of my house. I need to share with them the unsettling news of Jasmine's untimely death. More than that, though—after what's happened to her and Mia, I think we may need to put more restrictions on coming and going... And maybe even start instituting drug testing to keep members of the Family from both danger and succumbing to some of the evils of society—"

"I agree." Juan nodded. "I'll get on it."

"Good." Kenneth patted the shoulder of his most loyal follower, with Siobhan, his current bedmate, a close second. He would need them both while navigating troubled waters in the riverscape.

THAT AFTERNOON, STEFANIE sat in a booth with Bella at the Reston Hills River Pub on Third Street, as they sipped on mojitos.

"It sucks," Stefanie admitted, laying her sorrows out, not wanting to hold them in with the tragedy of Jasmine's death weighing on her.

"I know." Bella grimaced. "Especially since it seemed like Jasmine had something on her mind when she agreed to meet with you and Campbell. Someone must have wanted to prevent that meeting from ever taking place..."

"Right?" Stefanie sighed. "She was suspicious about Kenneth Braison—if not the entire Braison Family. Yet Jasmine was either too afraid or too brainwashed in the cult to break away altogether." Stefanie took a drink.

"Isn't that how it goes with these cults?" Bella pointed out. "They say all the right things to rope you in—perhaps convince you to give up your life savings and self-respect—then mess up your mind so you lose sight of what's right and what's wrong. If Jasmine—and maybe Mia as well—had decided they had enough of the Braison Family, that might have been the catalyst for Kenneth going after them. If it turns out that Jasmine, like Mia, died from a drug overdose, this will prove my point."

"Mine, too," Stefanie concurred, thinking about the conditions of which both died. "Both were without clothing, as if to make some type of morbid statement from their deaths to anyone else who would dare go against the cult..." Would Campbell reach the same conclusion? Or was there more to the story of the disturbing victimization than met the eye?

Bella tasted her cocktail and commented, "It is a bit bizarre... Just like it was when Lynda Boxleitner was found dead in a similar fashion on Founder's Day twenty years ago. It rocked the community and had people whispering and pointing fingers at the Braison Family. And even though Wendell Braison managed to avoid prosecution for the homicide, many people—including Mason Sawyer—never believed him to be innocent. The same may be true for his son, Kenneth Braison, who's fiercely protective of the Braison Family brand, whatever that entailed. The apple never falls too far from the tree, as the saying goes..."

"That's what they say," Stefanie agreed, though she was striving to keep an open mind as more details unfolded regarding Jasmine's death. "We'll just have to see what the investigation uncovers and just how deep within the Braison Family this could go—if anywhere at all."

Bella nodded. "I'm sure that Campbell and the entire police department are committed to doing their job and reaching the proper conclusions—whatever they happen to be and however long it takes—while giving the citizens of Reston Hills some much needed resolution to this unwelcome drama that they can live with."

"You're right about that," Stefanie said, offering her a smile of mutual support. "I need to take a step back and give Campbell the space he needs to figure this out."

"Probably a good idea." Bella held her hand. "You're my best friend, Stefanie. The last thing I want is to see you swept up in the Braison Family deeds and misdeeds—putting you in any type of danger."

Stefanie squeezed her hand, happy to see that she felt that way about her in such a short period of time since taking up residence in Reston Hills. "I feel the same way about you—we're besties," she told her.

"Nice to know." Bella's eyes lit up and she lifted her glass for a toast. "Cheers."

"Cheers." Stefanie grinned. She thought about her feelings for Campbell, which went well beyond camaraderie—and was sure he recognized this and was on the same wavelength. Beyond that, she would take any real friendship she could get in this new environment. Even if it meant sharing Bella with anyone she chose to romance, such as her current beau, Russell Kercheval, whom she insisted was only a work-in-progress at the moment.

Bella finished off her drink and said, "Next round's on me."

"You're on," Stefanie agreed, more than happy to take her thoughts off Jasmine and the sad way she'd ended up—dead in the park.

Chapter Fourteen

On Monday morning, Mason took his favorite quarter horse, Dodge, out for a solo ride. Sally was at work, but probably wishing she was away from her desk at a local publishing house on the south side of town and riding with him as she loved to do. He loved spending as much time with her as possible. Maybe they would get hitched someday. Or maybe it was best not to mess up a good thing while still holding on to the memory of his late wife, Alyssa.

As he rode down the trail with his well-worn Stetson hat on tightly, Mason couldn't help but wonder about his son's love life. He wouldn't mind seeing Campbell settle down and marry someone who could appreciate what he had to offer, and vice versa, while maybe bringing children into the world to keep the bloodline going and making him a doting granddad.

His mind turned to the cold case that the murder of Lynda Boxleitner had turned into after all these years. It still bugged him that he hadn't solved the case. He was sure that the answers were staring him right in the face. Only he had been unable to visualize what he was seeing.

He imagined the same was true with Campbell, who was busy trying to piece together his own cases of strange deaths involving naked young women. The latest one that was found at Reston Hills Park with similar characteristics was obviously patterned after the OD death of Mia O'Dell. What was that all about? Were both women simply drug addicts who were given a bad batch of drugs? Or was something more sinister at play here?

And did either death have anything to do with what happened to Lynda and the commonality involving the Braison Family? Or had the passage of time meant that the similarities were just strangely coincidental rather than someone with an agenda in mind to bridge the gap in the deaths?

As he headed back toward the house, Mason intended to take another hard look at his case files on Lynda's murder and, once again, see if anything stood out that might give him a new sense of direction. Perhaps he could help Campbell in his current investigation.

CAMPBELL WAS AT his desk, with Georgina standing over him, as Jennie Napier, the forensic pathologist, was visible on the screen of his laptop to provide them with the autopsy results on Jasmine Roxburgh.

"What do you have for us?" Campbell asked intently, sensing what she might say.

Adjusting her glasses, Jennie responded evenly, "Similar to the recent autopsy on Mia O'Dell, the decedent, twenty-five-year-old Jasmine Roxburgh, died from acute fentanyl intoxication—or fentanyl bromazolam, diazepam toxicity—the result of overdosing on a lethal amount of fentanyl mixed with its analog, carfentanil."

Campbell's brow furrowed, though she had confirmed his suspicions. "I have reason to believe that Ms. Roxburgh—a friend of Ms. O'Dell—was not doing drugs. Much less, fentanyl or carfentanil," he said, leaning on Stefanie's observation and intuition regarding the cult member. "That suggests to me that someone may have knowingly given Jasmine the fentanyl concoction for the purpose of killing her…"

Georgina pitched in, "It's hard to fathom that someone who just lost a friend to fentanyl would willingly follow in her footsteps by OD'ing herself."

"I understand where you're coming from." Jennie twisted her lips thoughtfully. "I'm assuming you share the same suspicions about Ms. O'Dell's fatal overdose being a case of outright murder?"

"How could we not," Campbell replied matter-of-factly, "given the similarities in the way they died—naked and in the park…" He peered at the forensic pathologist. "What can you tell us about the external condition of Jasmine's body?"

Jennie responded levelly, "The decedent had some scratches on her arms and legs, and blisters on her feet—as well as some bruising on her upper body, suggesting a physical struggle with someone in the process."

Campbell interpolated, "Someone that Jasmine may have been trying to escape from, but failed before, during, or after the fentanyl went to work on her system—in what amounts to, at the very least, a drug-induced homicide?" *If not cold-blooded murder*, he thought.

"Yes, that would be my thinking on the decedent's final minutes of life," Jennie said solemnly.

"Were there any signs of sexual assault?" Georgina asked interestedly.

"No—none that we could ascertain during the examination," she said.

Campbell took note of this, which lined up with the same confirmation in Mia's autopsy—that she hadn't been raped or otherwise sexually victimized. This indicated to him that neither Braison Family member was targeted for sexual criminality. But may well have been targeted for their common association with a cult and any attempts by the women to reject the teachings or conformity to the status quo.

When the conversation on the autopsy results ended, Georgina looked at Campbell and asked, "So, what do you think?"

He held her gaze and took a breath, before answering bluntly, "Someone obviously wanted both Jasmine and Mia dead for one reason or another..." Campbell mulled this over. "We could be looking at a serial killer—inside or outside the Braison Family."

Georgina's brow shot up. "You think so?"

Knowing that the FBI defined two killings at minimum—with as many as three when counting Lynda Boxleitner's death—as constituting serial murder when certain characteristics were present, which this qualified as in Campbell's book, he responded. "It's certainly something we need to consider, given the manner of death and discovery of Jasmine and Mia in less than a week—as though a serial killer's modus operandi—as an indicator that this is just getting started."

"Hmm...that's a scary thought," Georgina uttered, jutting her chin.

"I know, right?" Campbell sat back in his chair, pondering the concept. "While we need to keep an open mind on all possibilities, Kenneth Braison remains at the top of the list of suspects as the killer—serial or not—for either directly supplying and/or administering the lethal drugs or through his powerful reach with loyal and obedient followers as the head of the Braison Family."

Georgina sighed. "Meaning, whichever way we slice it, we still have our work cut out for us if we're to prevent more lethal overdoses...and homicides."

"Yeah, agreed." Campbell was blown over at the parallel thoughts, unsettling as they were. Moreover, he was determined to keep the deaths from going beyond the Braison Family members—with Stefanie being his greatest concern in that respect, as someone who had inadvertently been touched by Mia and Jasmine. In this instance, he saw that as a negative that a killer might see fit to use against Stefanie.

MASON SAT AT his desk while Hopper sat in front of the picture window, staring out at the meadow.

With all the information, statements, photographs and whatever else he had been able to keep as a cold case reminder of what had eluded him as a police detective taking up much of his desk space and some of the floor—Mason went through it all once more, hoping to find the proverbial needle in a haystack.

Sipping black coffee, he bit back on the frustrations at seemingly going around in circles. Just as had been the case twenty years ago. *Maybe I wasn't meant to ever fill in the blanks*, Mason surmised. Could be that some things in life were better left in the past.

He didn't believe that to be the case in this instance. Especially when the past and present had merged as though time had stood still. If Lynda's death was related in any way to the recent cult-related deaths, Mason sincerely believed it was incumbent upon him to lend his son a helping hand. And put his own mind at ease for the bargain.

As Mason went through the main suspects in Lynda's murder, he focused primarily on Wendell Braison, who'd had her under his thumb and in his bed as part of the cult manipulation and seemed more than capable of taking Lynda out if she crossed him. Or wanted out, if this went against his wishes.

But Braison was clever enough to keep from being boxed into a corner. They couldn't lay a finger on him in terms of an arrest and conviction.

Mason took another look at his son, Kenneth Braison. He was supposed to have been in Boise when Lynda was poisoned to death. But what if he had doubled back to commit the deed? Wendell would have done anything to shield his son from trouble—including paying off as many people as he needed to cover for him.

Studying the material, Mason wasn't feeling it about Kenneth being the culprit in Lynda's death, for whatever reason. Which didn't mean he wasn't responsible for the recent deaths of his followers in the Braison Family.

Mason turned to another suspect, Roger Pennock. A forty-nine-year-old professor, he was seen flirting with Lynda at Harriette's Café, where she worked part-time as a waitress, the day before her death. He was cleared after it was determined that he was in the hospital being treated for a peptic ulcer during Lynda's estimated time of death.

Similarly, Howard Henesy, a thirty-six-year-old homeless veteran, who was found lurking near Reston Hills

Park just after midnight on Founder's Day in the vicinity of where Lynda's body was found, was dropped as a suspect when it was discovered that he'd solicited the services of a local prostitute—the two spending more than an hour together smoking marijuana and having sex, around the time of Lynda's death.

Mason sipped his coffee and sighed, nearly ready to call it quits on what was starting to look like a futile attempt at unlocking the past, when he came across another name that barely registered.

Sidney Sedwick.

Mason saw that Sedwick was forty-two at the time and worked as a gardener for Stuart Reston, whom Mason had done some off-duty security work for himself from time to time for extra pay outside of police work. Looking deeper at his notes, he noted that Sedwick had been seen with Lynda in his Ford F-150 pickup days before she was killed. He claimed he was only giving her a lift as a friend.

Sedwick's solid alibi for Lynda's death was that he was working with other volunteers all night on Founder's Day preparations. Many vouched for him. Moreover, Stuart Reston backed Sedwick as a hard worker with not a bad bone in his body. Given Stuart's stature in the town that bore his family's surname, this carried a lot of weight in looking elsewhere beyond Sedwick—who had no criminal record—for a killer.

But now Mason found himself revisiting the former gardener as a possible suspect in Lynda's death. Was his relationship with Lynda truly only platonic in nature? Or was there something more to it, such as sexual, at a time when Sedwick was divorced and lived alone?

As Hopper got up and made his way over to him,

Mason couldn't help but think that, as a gardener, Sidney Sedwick may have had access to the poisonous rodenticide and insecticide, thallium sulfate, that Lynda died from. Though the tasteless, odorless and colorless pesticide had been banned for decades at the time in the United States, it was still available and accessible in some other countries.

Could Sedwick have gotten his hands on some and used it on Lynda? Moreover, could he have graduated from thallium sulfate to fentanyl…and picked up where he left off in lethal poisonings of women in Reston Hills?

Mason chewed on these disturbing thoughts.

CAMPBELL SAT ON a mesh-back side chair in Chief Gloria Schecter's office as he briefed her on the latest—and no less disturbing—death to hit Reston Hills Park.

"This might be the work of a serial killer—possibly spanning two decades," he told her, bothered by the prospect.

Seated at her desk, Gloria's eyes widened behind her glasses. "Go on…"

Campbell sighed. "According to the autopsy findings, Jasmine Roxburgh's death was caused by acute fentanyl intoxication—or a lethal overdose of fentanyl combined with carfentanil—the same as Mia O'Dell. Both were found in the park naked—which, in and of itself is highly suspicious, even if they were under some delusional state from the effects of the fentanyl poisoning. The fact that they were members of the Braison Family—much like Lynda Boxleitner, who, as you know, had no clothes on when she died at the same location twenty years ago, albeit from thallium sulfate poisoning—suggests that the deaths are linked to the cult either by association or by someone who has it out for the followers…"

"Hmm…" Gloria pursed her lips. "If it's true that we're dealing with a poisonous serial killer, then it would effectively exonerate Wendell Braison in the unsolved death of Boxleitner," she threw out. "Am I right?"

Campbell considered this for a beat. "Yeah, that would seem to be the case—assuming we're talking about the same killer of all three women…" He paused. "It's still possible that Braison killed Lynda Boxleitner and someone else—perhaps Kenneth Braison—has taken up the cause, ritual, retaliation or whatever in using fentanyl to kill Jasmine Roxburgh and Mia O'Dell. We're not ruling anything out at the moment," he emphasized.

"Nor should you." Gloria leaned forward and said, "Keep digging and see what you unearth. If these are serial homicides—especially two decades in the making—we may need to bring the FBI in on this investigation. Given our somewhat limited resources, any help would always be welcome."

Maybe not always, Campbell thought, knowing the penchant the Bureau had to want to take the lead in any investigation they were involved in. Still, he wasn't so territorial that he would turn his back on their assistance, if offered. But first, he wanted more clarity as to whether he was onto something about the serial killer angle. Or if it was possible that Mia's and Jasmine's deaths were simply fatal drug overdoses that had landed them in the park—with the nudity merely a reflection of their affiliation with the Braison Family and being comfortable with no clothes on for the freedom it gave them.

IN HER STUDIO, Stefanie led the way in a Yin yoga class, which focused on stretching exercises, as part of the mind-body routines she offered. The attendees, including two men, seemed all in with her instructions and were following her lead nicely. Bella was there in her designer yoga wear, flashing a brilliant smile, and had no trouble keeping up.

Stefanie sucked in a measured breath. Frankly, she welcomed taking her attention away from the Braison Family and the mysterious deaths of their two followers. At the same time, she wanted Campbell to figure it all out and—if he could prove that Kenneth Braison or anyone else was at the center of the fatal poisonings—put the mystery to rest. And presumably prevent any other cult members from dying due to a drug overdose.

She returned her thoughts to the yoga class, feeling good about having brought her skills and knowledge on this and tai chi to Reston Hills. Maybe she could talk Campbell into attending one class or the other, even if he obviously needed no help whatsoever in the fitness department—in or out of bed. It would still give them another opportunity to bond in her world, as a measure of spending time together for whatever the future might bring. Beyond that, she imagined that he would even enjoy the classes, which were designed to be fun as much as healthy exercising. It was also something that would give Campbell a probably much-needed breather of his own from the tricky world of law enforcement and the challenges that undoubtedly came with the territory.

Chapter Fifteen

"I may have a lead on my cold case—or actually yours now..." Mason said over the phone.

Campbell, who was still at his desk, responded attentively, "Okay, what do you have?"

Without elaborating, his father said flatly, "Can you meet me at Sedwick's Greenhouse and Nursery on Bledton Road in Wally Ridge?"

"Yeah, sure," Campbell told him. "I can be there in about twenty minutes."

"See you then."

Campbell heard the phone disconnect. He finished up some paperwork and headed out of the building, stepping into the sunshine, while more than curious as to where this was headed. Not too surprisingly, his father had taken an active interest in the unofficial reopening of the Lynda Boxleitner homicide.

Had he made a breakthrough?

Campbell was just as keen to solve the decades-old murder. Especially if it was connected to the two current drug-related deaths he was investigating. After getting into his SUV, he sent Stefanie a quick text to say that he was thinking about her—and often. A return text came back from her, stating the same was true from her end.

It brought a smile to his face as he realized how good it felt to have someone like her that enjoyed his company and wanted more of it.

He drove off to the rural town in Eckerslin County—about halfway between Reston Hills and Fallon's Creek. Spotting his father's Land Rover Range Rover in the parking lot of Sedwick's Greenhouse and Nursery, Campbell parked alongside him.

After climbing into the passenger side of his father's luxury SUV, he said, "Hey."

"Hey." Mason, wearing his cowboy hat, turned to face Campbell. "I've been going through my old files, hoping to find something…anything that might catch my eye…" He drew a breath. "Something did click. I came across info on one of the original suspects in Lynda's murder… His name's Sidney Sedwick—"

Campbell strained his mind to recall the name through his own perusal of the cold case files. He seemed to remember that Sedwick was barely mentioned, with the focus being almost entirely on Wendell Braison.

"I remember the name Sidney Sedwick," Campbell said, leaving it at that for now.

"Sedwick was employed at the time as a gardener by Stuart Reston," Mason pointed out, piquing Campbell's interest with the mention of Bella Reston's late father. "A witness reported seeing Lynda riding with Sedwick in his Ford F-150 pickup just days before her body was found in the park."

"Hmm…" Campbell muttered thoughtfully. "Where was Sedwick—or where was he supposed to be—when she was killed?"

"According to witnesses, he spent the entire night before Founder's Day into the early morning hours working on preparations for the event, apparently giving him no time to poison Lynda. Beyond that, Stuart came to Sedwick's defense—insisting that he was a stand-up guy, incapable of doing anyone harm."

Campbell eyed his father. "What made you think—or reconsider—otherwise?"

Mason ran a hand across his mouth. "Well, although Sedwick came back clean in a criminal background check, the fact that he was a gardener and may have been able to get his hands on the pesticide used to fatally poison Lynda just stuck out with me this time around."

"What about his alibi?" Campbell asked as he weighed this.

"Yeah, there is that," Mason admitted. "But from my own volunteering for past Founder's Day planning, I know firsthand that it can be chaotic. People come and go without anyone truly being the wiser—but would swear that someone never left their sight."

Campbell cocked a brow. "So, you think that Sedwick could have slipped away, poisoned Lynda, dumped her in Reston Hills Park and returned to the Founder's Day preparations unnoticed?"

"Maybe." Mason sighed. "Guess I'd like to hear what Sedwick has to say about it twenty years later—if he'll talk to us... I did some digging, made some phone calls and learned that he now owns this greenhouse and nursery."

Campbell nodded. "Well, let's go see if we can find him."

"Okay."

They walked inside the greenhouse and, after asking to

see Sidney Sedwick, were directed toward the perennials department. A medium-sized man in his early sixties with a silver Viking haircut and a Balbo beard was getting his hands dirty on some shrubs when they approached him.

Flashing his badge, Campbell took the initial lead. "I'm Detective Sawyer, Reston Hills Police Department."

Mason said evenly in a throwback, "I'm Detective Sawyer, too, and his father. Are you Sidney Sedwick?"

His shoulders slouched and his brown eyes narrowed while responding, "Yeah, that's me."

"We've spoken before," Mason told him matter-of-factly. "Twenty years ago…about the murder of Lynda Boxleitner—"

Sidney nodded. "I remember. How could I not?"

Campbell told him straightforwardly, "The case has been reopened… We'd like to ask you a few questions about it…" Even then, he was sizing up the suspect, wondering if he could be responsible as well for the deaths of Jasmine and Mia. "Is there somewhere we can talk?"

Sidney took a breath and replied, "Yeah—my office…"

They followed him back through the greenhouse and into a small windowless office with a standing desk workstation, wooden square table and two leather chairs.

Mason peered at the suspect and asked point-blank, "Is there something you'd like to get off your chest after all these years? Did you kill Lynda Boxleitner?"

Sidney stared at the question for a long moment. He sighed, then said levelly, "No, I did not kill Lynda… Had an alibi. And I could never have done that—"

"But she was in your truck days before her death," Mason said tersely.

Sidney freely admitted, "Yeah, I gave her a lift…"

Campbell sensed that he was holding back, prompting him to ask, "Do you know who could have poisoned her to death?"

Before he could respond, Mason put forth stridently, "As a gardener, you might have had knowledge of and access to thallium sulfate—the banned pesticide someone used to fatally poison Lynda. Maybe you chose to use it on her, for whatever reason…?" Mason glared at him and said, "Maybe you're at it again?"

Sidney's head snapped back as if he had been punched. He paused, then said thoughtfully, "There are some things I need to get off my chest. I've wanted to for a long time. Guess I was just waiting for you to show up—" he eyed Mason "—to say what should have been said twenty years ago…"

Campbell exchanged a curious glance with his father, both wondering, no doubt, if Sidney Sedwick was about to have second thoughts and confess to the murder of Lynda Boxleitner, for starters…

Sidney sucked in a deep breath, jutted his chin and said, "I was able to obtain some thallium sulfate from abroad… But not for myself. I got it for Stuart Reston."

"Stuart—" Mason lifted a brow with surprise. "What are you saying?"

"I'm saying that Mr. Reston asked me to order it…said he thought the pesticide might be more effective in dealing with a pest problem that was getting out of control on the property than what we were using."

Campbell contemplated this, then asked the obvious question, "Did Stuart Reston know Lynda Boxleitner?"

"Yeah, he knew her," Sidney said without hesitating.

"How well did he know her?" Mason asked pointedly.

"They were having an affair." Sidney's voice rose an octave. "Mr. Reston was sleeping with Lynda right under the nose of his wife, Eloise Reston, and their daughter, Bella. Or maybe not so much. You see, Mr. Reston often had me pick up and drive Lynda to various meeting places behind Mrs. Reston's and Bella's back. Sometimes he and Lynda even got together at my cottage. But from what I'd heard, Lynda wanted more than what he was offering her in their arrangement—I don't know, maybe to become the next Mrs. Reston—to keep her from letting the whole world know about their illicit affair. Mr. Reston, with too much to lose in this town, would have none of it."

Campbell narrowed his eyes as he digested this. "Are you saying that it was Reston who killed her—his lover?"

Sidney licked his lips and responded, "He never came right out and confessed to it—though I asked him if he used the thallium sulfate to kill her—but sidestepped it, saying it was better if I didn't know. He paid me to keep quiet, which I did. Knowing it was in my best interests not to cross him, I've stayed silent till this day…"

Mason cast him a firm look. "If you're leveling with us, you really believe neither Eloise nor Bella had a clue that Stuart was fooling around with Lynda…?"

"I never got that impression," Sidney claimed, "from when I was around them—which wasn't very often. I think that, being as clever as he was, Mr. Reston was able to pull the wool over their eyes about this."

Campbell took a step closer and asked pensively, "Do you recall how Reston felt about Lynda being a member of the Braison Family?"

"Yeah, I remember. He wasn't that thrilled about it, but it was her life." Sidney pulled on his beard. "Mr. Reston didn't care much for the cult—believing they were simply brainwashing gullible followers. Including Lynda. I guess he was happy to have her whenever he could—which wasn't as often as he would have liked, given his other obligations."

Mason set his jaw. "Since Stuart Reston is no longer around to defend himself from your insinuation and you admit to being the one to illegally bring thallium sulfate into this country, why should we believe Reston used the poison to kill Lynda—and not you—the so-called alibi notwithstanding...?"

Sidney sucked in a deep breath and answered unwaveringly, "Because this has been eating away at me for the past two decades and I gain nothing from lying. I liked Lynda, even if I didn't really know her all that well. She didn't deserve to end up like she did at the park that Founder's Day." His mouth tightened. "If Mr. Reston didn't poison her, he had the means to get someone else to do his dirty work. But it wasn't me."

Campbell looked at his father and Mason held his gaze, both contemplative in that unexpected moment of revelation.

HE FOLLOWED HIS father's SUV to Harriette's Café, which Mason had introduced Campbell to as a boy when his father was still on the force. They needed to talk about what Sidney Sedwick had confessed to. Or more precisely what he hadn't taken ownership of. He had pointed the finger squarely at Bella's father, Stuart Reston, as the person responsible for Lynda Boxleitner's death.

In Campbell's mind, this implication completely upended the belief that Wendell Braison had murdered

Lynda. Whether she was romantically involved with him too was immaterial. Given Sedwick's role in supplying Reston with the thallium sulfate—in combination with his alleged infidelity with Lynda and possible blackmail on her part—it wasn't too much of a stretch to think that Reston, with much to lose in his marriage and position in society, might have chosen a deadly way out of his dilemma. And used Sidney Sedwick to achieve his goals.

Wonder how Dad is feeling about this sudden twist in a cold case? Campbell asked himself. He also couldn't help but wonder if Bella had ever suspected that her father was cheating on her mother. If so, there was no indication that she had ever held it against him, typically speaking of Stuart Reston in glowing terms—similar to her grandfather, Malcolm Reston, and great-grandfather, Arthur Reston. Or maybe she simply chose to judge her father for the good contributions he'd made to Reston Hills and not the bad.

Campbell pulled into the parking lot and caught up to his dad as they went inside the café.

They took a seat at the counter, and Sarah Huffstetler quickly came over to fill their coffee mugs. "Hey, handsome," she said with a big smile to Campbell.

He blushed. "Hey, Sarah."

She turned to Mason and said, "And another handsome gentleman, too."

"My father," Campbell told her proudly.

"Hey," Mason said, a small grin playing on his lips.

"Hi there." Sally put a hand on her hip, studying them. "I can see the resemblance."

"Not surprised." Campbell smiled at her, then waited for her to leave them alone.

Mason watched as she walked away, then eyed his son. "Is there something you want to tell me?"

"Yeah, since you ask—I am seeing someone," Campbell took the opportunity to reveal. "Only it's not Sarah."

Mason lifted a brow. "Oh?"

Campbell tasted the coffee. "Her name's Stefanie. She's a yoga and tai chi instructor in town." *And so much more*, he thought. "We met on Founder's Day."

"Uh-huh," Mason muttered thoughtfully, putting the coffee cup to his lips. "The same day that Mia O'Dell's body was discovered?"

"Stefanie was the one who found her on the trail in the park," Campbell noted. "We've been in each other's lives ever since."

His father nodded. "Good to hear. Hope this one works out."

"Me too." Campbell smiled when thinking about Stefanie. "I have a feeling she's the real deal."

Mason grinned. "Look forward to meeting her."

"You will," Campbell promised. He drank coffee and turned his thoughts to the visit with Stuart Reston's former gardener. "What do you make of what Sidney Sedwick had to say? Are you buying any of it?"

"I have to admit, Sedwick's bombshell sort of came out of left field." Mason rested an arm on the counter. "I went to the greenhouse hoping to extract a confession out of him, two decades removed—not have Sedwick claim that it was Stuart Reston who used poison to kill Lynda, after having an affair with her." Mason sipped his coffee. "When I did some work for Stuart, he seemed to be a bona fide family man who loved his wife. But looks can always be deceiving. Especially if Stuart wanted to present a false picture for obvious reasons. Lynda wasn't the same person I dated in high school at that stage. But she was still nice looking and she brought something to the table that might have enticed Stuart enough to go after her."

Campbell finished his coffee and asked probingly, "So, where does this leave Wendell Braison as a suspect in Lynda's murder?"

Mason considered this while closing his eyes for a moment, before regarding him and replying candidly, "It turns what I thought I knew about the man upside down. And turns my thoughts on Stuart right side up. Or, in other words, I'm starting to believe I had it all wrong that Braison killed Lynda—with Stuart Reston now taking up that position as a killer…"

Campbell was of the same view on Reston topping the list of suspects, though Sidney Sedwick's word alone wouldn't be enough to close the books on Lynda Boxleitner's murder.

Nor did it tell Campbell who was responsible for supplying Mia O'Dell and Jasmine Roxburgh with deadly fentanyl in what amounted to serial murder, through one deliberate action or another.

THAT NIGHT, IN her bed with Campbell, Stefanie was still reeling after being told about the suspicions that Bella's father, Stuart Reston, had poisoned Lynda Boxleitner, his alleged lover. Stuart's former gardener was apparently credible enough that both Campbell and his father, Mason Sawyer, were sold on the notion enough that Wendell Braison was no longer at the top of the list of suspects in Lynda's murder.

Stefanie wondered where this left Kenneth Braison as a

suspect in being the mastermind—if not actual culprit—of the drug-induced deaths of Jasmine and Mia. Were the cold case and current cases now thought to be unrelated?

"Do you think that Bella could've known her father was having an affair with Lynda—if, in fact, he was?" Campbell asked curiously as Stefanie rested her head on his firm chest.

She lifted her chin musingly. "Probably not. I think most cheating parents go to great lengths to keep it a secret," she told him. "Especially from their children, who would then be put in a rather awkward position as to whether or not to reveal this to the other parent."

"Maybe best if she didn't know—which would have meant knocking Stuart Reston off whatever pedestal she had him on." Campbell sighed. "Unfortunately, the cat may need to be let out of the bag—no disrespect to your wonderful cat, Curlie," he quipped. "If we get anything else concrete on the Boxleitner homicide that can tie it directly to Stuart Reston, it will have to made public—the town's namesake or not."

"I understand," Stefanie said acceptingly. She just wondered if Bella would. "So, do you still feel that the Braison Family is behind Jasmine's and Mia's deaths?"

With his arm wrapped around her, Campbell waited a beat and responded, "That's still open for consideration—but, as of now, there's reason enough to believe that someone within the cult's orbit is involved in the fatal fentanyl poisonings. Question is who—and to what degree? If not Kenneth Braison, then another cult member…" Campbell ran a hand along her bare shoulder. "Beyond that, it's not far reaching to think that they could have a serial killer in their midst—if not outside of the Family—on a deadly mission of targeting followers—"

"Hmm," Stefanie murmured reflectively while taking comfort being in Campbell's much-needed company. She thought about Mia and Jasmine and who could be next if an unidentified killer was roaming free to poison Braison Family members one by one.

Chapter Sixteen

The next day, Campbell sat inside his Chevy Tahoe in the police department lot. He was looking at his laptop, requesting a video chat with FBI Special Agent Rudi Villanueva, based in the Bureau's resident agency in Boise. She happened to be a criminal profiler who specialized in serial killers, whom he had worked with in joint task force investigations when he was with the Boise Police Department.

When Rudi accepted the call, her heart-shaped face appeared on the screen. In her late thirties, she was green-eyed and had blond hair in a whisper pixie. "Hey, Sawyer," she said cheerfully.

Campbell grinned. "Good morning, Rudi."

"How's life treating you in Reston Hills?"

Great on the romance front, he thought, but that wasn't the purpose of his call. So he responded frankly, "Not as well as I'd like these days..."

"Oh?" Her eyes widened. "What's up?"

Campbell told her about the two fentanyl-mixed-with-carfentanil fatalities connected to a cult, including the victims both found in the nude, with no indication of being sexually assaulted. Though it appeared as if the deaths were unrelated to the two decades old murder of

Lynda Boxleitner, it seemed worth throwing it into the mix, given the notable similarities.

"I'm wondering if the overdoses, coming so close to one another at the same park, could be something more than the supplying of fentanyl and its analog as a drug-induced homicide," Campbell put out. "Such as the deliberate actions of a serial killer operating inside or outside of the Braison Family cult—possibly for years…?"

Rudi contemplated the info he'd shared with her for a minute or two, digesting it as her profiler side kicked into gear, before responding coolly, "Aside from the realities of the fentanyl epidemic and its devastating impact on communities across the country, these scenarios you've laid out are certainly thought-provoking." She drew a breath. "So, without having more time to delve into the deaths and their characteristics, with respect to fatal ODs, there does seem to be some symmetry between the two recent deaths and the death twenty years ago—which isn't to say they are directly related or orchestrated by the same person. That being said, the cult angle is interesting."

"Okay," Campbell said after hanging on her every word. "How much so?"

"Well, by its very nature, a cult is typically associated with a religious group of sorts that indoctrinates its followers to buying in to whatever philosophy they're selling—usually going against the grain of mainstream society and, at times, drifting into questionable or aberrant behavior." Rudi sighed. "Anyway, based on what you've told me, the way I see it, there are likely two strong possibilities here relative to serial murder… The first is that the two recent drug-related deaths are ritualistic killings by the cult in a ceremonial method of maintaining control over their followers—which, if true, would still qualify as serial homicides."

She ran a hand through her hair and continued, "The second, and probably most likely possibility, is that someone today—either within the Braison Family or not— was influenced by the Founder's Day homicide from twenty years ago. So there is a copycat killer deliberately mimicking it or pretending it's the same killer to perhaps throw you off from the real agenda, while substituting the thallium sulfate for the more accessible fentanyl to carry out the killings."

Campbell peered at the screen and stated, if hearing her words correctly, "So, the unsub—if there is one—is probably reenacting the murder of cult member Lynda Boxleitner as a smokescreen to perpetrate the modern-day cult-related killings of Mia O'Dell and Jasmine Roxburgh with another motive in mind?"

"That's where I would go with this and what you need to figure out," Rudi suggested. "Of course, there's always the possibility—slim as it might be—that a cold case killer has lay in wait for two decades, till the opportunity came to resume Braison Family members."

"Hmm..." Campbell weighed that angle. His current belief was that Stuart Reston had likely been the one to use thallium sulfate to kill his lover, Lynda Boxleitner. Thus, there was little reason to think that someone else—perhaps who had been incarcerated for another crime or otherwise prevented from acting out—had chosen to target followers of Kenneth Braison. Campbell preferred to believe that a killer was motivated to kill based on present circumstances and not past ones. "We'll see where this goes," he said. "Appreciate your thoughts."

Rudi smiled. "Always happy to help whenever I can." She paused. "Good luck with your investigation."

"Thanks." Campbell ended the video chat. He certainly wasn't counting on luck to solve this, but he was happy to accept it nevertheless. He closed the lid to the laptop and went inside the building.

"Stuart Reston?" Gloria's mouth stayed open in shock, as she stood in the conference room, which had a curved big-screen monitor, a rectangular wooden meeting table and leather chairs with wheels.

"Yeah, looks like he could have killed Lynda Boxleitner," Campbell reiterated, standing beside her, after giving the chief and Georgina, along with other detectives sitting around the table—including one from the Cold Case Unit—the rundown on what he and his father had gotten out of Reston's former gardener, Sidney Sedwick. "If Sedwick is to be believed—and his argument was pretty persuasive, I must admit—he got his hands on some thallium sulfate at the request of Reston, who used it to poison Boxleitner, his lover—presumably to keep their tryst from being exposed, as she may have threatened to do."

Gloria sighed. "Reston wasn't even on our radar as a suspect, which I'm sure Mason told you," she said, her voice rising an octave.

"He did," Campbell acknowledged, hoping his dad wouldn't be blamed for missing the boat here. "Guess Reston's prominent position in town and even apparently having an alibi of being with his wife, Eloise Reston, at the time Lynda Boxleitner was killed was more than enough to keep him from being looked at strongly as a suspect. And Sedwick had an alibi as well that held up." Campbell suddenly felt the need to defend his father's original investigation. "Whereas Wendell Braison—whom Lynda was also linked to romantically and as a member of the Braison Family cult—was a more likely person of interest in her death, given the manner in which she died and other circumstantial evidence that pointed in Braison's direction."

Gloria nodded and said thoughtfully, "Sedwick's accusations, serious as they are, against a deceased Stuart Reston—in which Sedwick admits to being complicit in obtaining the poison used to kill Boxleitner—may not be enough to reopen the investigation formally. But it does give us good reason to take the onus off Wendell Braison, with the long-held belief that he had gotten away with murder."

"I agree," Campbell said, even if he wasn't quite ready to say the same for Kenneth Braison, who was still a suspect in the current investigation.

Ulrich González, the slim thirtysomething, brown-eyed cold case detective, whose black hair was in a military-style undercut, looked at him and then the chief before saying, "I'd be happy to do some more digging into this if you like."

Campbell took the liberty of replying unenthusiastically, "Knock yourself out." He knew that it would ultimately be Gloria's call and doubted she would want to prioritize this ahead of other cold cases that had more to work with at this point in time. She didn't disappoint him in dissuading Ulrich from this.

Georgina leaned forward at the table and asked for further clarification, "With the Lynda Boxleitner murder moving in a different direction, where does that leave us in connecting it to the OD deaths of Jasmine Roxburgh and Mia O'Dell?"

"Glad you asked," Campbell told her with a slight grin. "I think the Boxleitner death inspired a copycat to use a currently available poison to kill O'Dell and Roxburgh in a manner that links all three deaths to the Braison Family." He sighed. "The degree of that linkage and whether or not it amounts to a serial killer at large in Reston Hills remains to be seen."

THAT AFTERNOON, CAMPBELL AND GEORGINA, along with armed detectives from the Reston Hills Police Department's Narcotics Unit, a SWAT team, K-9 unit's dual-purpose drug-detection canines, and US Drug Enforcement Administration special agents, converged on a ranch house on Quakely Road. Based on evidence that strongly suggested that the fentanyl powder mixed with the potent synthetic opioid fentanyl analog, carfentanil had come from a known purported local drug dealer named Luther Valdez, a search warrant was issued for his Reston Hills residence.

Valdez, fifty-six, had served a dozen years in federal prison for various drug-trafficking offenses. Now Campbell wondered if he was up to his old tricks, supplying the deadly drugs that killed Mia and Jasmine. Just as important was, if true, whether or not Valdez had sold the fentanyl directly to the victims. Or to someone else, who had chosen to commit serial murder.

Campbell noted that there were two vehicles parked on the property—a black Mitsubishi Outlander SUV that was registered to Valdez, and a red Honda Pilot Sport

SUV. The assumption was that the occupants of the house were armed, so they would act accordingly in executing the warrant.

Wearing a ballistic vest beneath his blazer, Campbell made contact with Georgina, also with a vest on, then the rest of the team, before giving the go-ahead for the raid to proceed.

Within moments, they had stormed the house. It had little in the way of furnishings—mostly traditional—with hardwood flooring. The citrusy scent of marijuana permeated the air as they were confronted by a Rottweiler guard dog. The K-9 unit was able to effectively deal with the threat by subduing the animal and safely removing it from the premises.

They detained, without further resistance, the sole occupant—a medium built, short male with textured brown hair in a mullet cut, a scruffy beard and dark eyes—who identified himself as Luther Valdez.

After presenting him with the warrant, the search of the residence ensued. Confiscated were illegal narcotics—including fentanyl pills in multiple colors, fentanyl powder and liquid, methamphetamine, heroin, and cocaine—and oxycodone, a painkiller. Also seized were illegal firearms and ammunition.

Valdez was taken into custody to face charges.

IN AN INTERROGATION ROOM, Campbell got the first crack at the suspect, before the Feds would ultimately take possession of him, seeing that a number of suspected serious drug-related violations of federal law had been made by Luther Valdez.

Sitting in a wooden chair across a metal table from the

suspect, Campbell glanced at the video camera that was recording the interview, then back at Valdez, and said to him in a deep tone of voice, "It looks like you had quite an operation going there." And obviously had not learned any lessons from his previous stint behind bars.

Valdez scratched his beard and muttered, "Yeah, I guess."

"Uh, this means you're in a lot of trouble," Campbell told him mockingly, in case he didn't get that. "Drug trafficking happens to be a serious crime in this state—and the country."

Valdez rolled his eyes. "So why am I here?"

"You're here because I'd like to help you, if you'll help me—" Campbell said, watching his reaction.

"How's that?" he asked suspiciously.

Campbell dodged the question. He pushed two pictures in front of his face and said solemnly, "Since Founder's Day, these two women have OD'd on fentanyl mixed with carfentanil… I have good reason to believe that the drugs came from you. The question is, did you sell or give it to them directly? Or did you sell it to someone else?" He considered that it was a leap of faith that they had zeroed in on the right drug trafficker. Now he only needed him to bite the bait.

Valdez studied the two faces of the dead women, taken after the fact for maximum effect on the results of drug overdoses. He jutted his chin and said tonelessly, "I've never seen either of them before."

Campbell wasn't sure he bought that, and pressed him. "Your drugs killed them," he said flatly. "If you didn't hand them a death sentence directly, then someone else did. Who did you sell the fentanyl powder laced with carfentanil to on or around Founder's Day?"

Valdez set his jaw. "What's in it for me?"

I was afraid he'd ask that, Campbell told himself. He responded straightforwardly, "If you're legit, I can put in a good word for you when your case moves forward. Could make the difference in how you fare at the end of the day. Now, I need a name." He wondered if Kenneth Braison's name would pop out of his mouth.

After a moment or two of contemplation, Valdez leaned toward him and said, "I sold the fentanyl to Juan Barrientos—"

"Barrientos?" Campbell hoisted a brow, glancing at the video camera.

"Yeah. We go back a ways. Juan said he needed it to help keep some people in line with that cult he belongs to…" Valdez rubbed his nose. "I only sold him the drug. How he chose to use it wasn't my call."

"You can't get off that easily," Campbell told him unsympathetically, as Valdez was just as culpable in knowing that fentanyl could be deadly. But right now, the onus was on Barrientos. Had he taken it upon himself to drug the women for one reason or another? Or had he acted on behalf of Kenneth Braison as a means to control his followers—whatever the costs? "When exactly did this drug transaction take place?" Campbell demanded of the drug trafficker.

"A day before Founder's Day," Valdez answered without runup. "Said he needed some of the stuff in a hurry."

Campbell sighed thoughtfully. If this was the real deal, Barrientos would be held accountable for his decision to perpetrate drug-induced homicides on Mia and Jasmine. As would the man who sold him the deadly drug. "We'll check out your story," he told him keenly. "And go from there…"

Valdez seemed content to let this play out, undoubtedly hoping it would work in his favor to one degree or another when he was handed over to federal authorities.

Fifteen minutes later, Campbell was at his desk, going over the claims by Valdez with Georgina, who was at her own desk.

"If Valdez is telling the truth about Barrientos, there's our smoking gun," Campbell said matter-of-factly, "with respect to linking Mia O'Dell and Jasmine Roxburgh's fatal ODs. The big question is what does Kenneth Braison know and how long has he known it?"

"Yeah, both need to be answered, sooner rather than later," Georgina said, staring at her laptop. "Valdez, the creep that he is, has basically pointed the finger at the Braison Family itself and their involvement through Barrientos in Roxburgh and O'Dell's deaths."

Campbell lowered his chin. "Now we need to make the case for this."

"I think I found something that backs Valdez up on his claim of selling the fentanyl to Barrientos—if only by connotation in Mia's fatal OD…" Georgina said. "Come take a look…"

Campbell got up and walked over to her desk. "What are we looking at?" he asked, watching the video over her shoulder.

"It's surveillance video we obtained from a security camera not far from where Mia O'Dell was last seen alive," she responded. "There's Mia…"

"I see her." Campbell stared at the small screen, waiting for more.

"Watch as the blue Volvo XC60 SUV pulls up alongside Mia," Georgina said anxiously. "She looks inside, says something, then gets into the passenger seat before the SUV drives off—toward the direction of Reston Hills Park."

Since he couldn't make out the driver of the vehicle, Campbell said, "Can you back that up and zoom in on the license plate?"

Georgina did so for his benefit while saying excitedly, "I'm already two steps ahead. I checked out the plate." She drew a breath. "The SUV's registered to Juan Barrientos—"

"We've got him," Campbell told her, feeling that the pieces had fallen into place that Barrientos had, in fact, lured Mia into his vehicle and gotten her to ingest the powdered fentanyl—before or after he took her to the park to leave her to die. The pattern fits as well in the death of Jasmine Roxburgh. Now they only needed to get him into custody and see just how far up the Braison Family chain this went.

Chapter Seventeen

Stefanie was a little surprised to see the door opened by Bella, after having come to expect that task to be done by her dependable, and seemingly always present, housekeeper, Nadine Marinkovich.

Bella grinned attractively. "Hey."

"Hey," Stefanie said, smiling back as she walked inside, paying her friend a planned visit just to chill out. "Where's Nadine?"

"I gave her the day off," Bella explained, as if feeling guilty for not doing so sooner. "Nadine works way too hard, cleaning up after me and my guests—present company excluded," she added with a laugh. "You're too much of a neat freak!"

Stefanie chuckled. "We are who we are," she said, taking ownership of what she assumed was a compliment.

"So true." Bella flashed her teeth. "Anyway, let's go sit in the den. I made herbal tea."

"Okay." Stefanie glanced toward the incredible kitchen with its luxury appliances, waterfall island and quartz countertops.

They got past the great room and formal dining room before entering the den. It was spacious, with white wood paneling, interlocking hardwood flooring, a vaulted ceiling, two matching upholstered swivel armchairs and a corduroy modular sectional.

Bella sat on the sectional sofa and waited for Stefanie to sit beside her, which she did. She handed Stefanie a cup of herbal tea from a bamboo serving tray on a farmhouse coffee table, and then picked up the other cup for herself.

"So, how's your day been?" Bella asked casually.

Stefanie sipped the tea, thoughtful. "Same old, same old."

"Anything new on the dual investigations?"

"Not really," Stefanie told her. *Should I mention anything about the allegations leveled at her father, that he was having an affair with Lynda Boxleitner, only to poison her to death?* she wondered before deciding it wasn't her place to do so.

Stefanie suspected that Bella, being as devoted as she was to her family, would deny any unproven insinuations against her father. The fact that he was now deceased made it highly unlikely that the truth would ever come out, one way or the other, in spite of his former gardener's accusations regarding the affair and Stuart's use of the toxic thallium sulfate to silence Lynda forever.

Stefanie tasted the tea. "Have you heard anything?" she asked nonchalantly.

"Nothing comes to mind," Bella said, putting the cup of tea to her glossed lips.

"Guess we'll just have to wait and see how things turn out," Stefanie suggested, knowing that whatever came out about Stuart Reston, Bella would just have to deal with it and, hopefully, get past it.

"Right." Bella sat her teacup down and watched as Stefanie sipped more. "Is the tea as good as I think it is?"

"Yes, excellent," Stefanie replied with a smile, tasting the blend of elderflower, chamomile and lemon.

Bella grinned. "Glad you like it." She waited a beat before taking a breath and saying evenly, "There's something I have to tell you, Stefanie... I've been wanting to talk about this with someone for the longest time, but it never quite seemed like the right time. Till now..."

"Okay." Stefanie regarded her, curious as to what was weighing on her friend's mind. "You've got my full attention."

"Thanks." Bella lifted her cup, took a sip and put it back on the tray. "Where do I begin?"

"Anywhere you're comfortable with," Stefanie prodded, and sipped the tea again before setting it down.

"All right. Here goes..." Bella sat back, thoughtful. "My father had an affair with Lynda Boxleitner—"

Stefanie raised an eyebrow. "Really?" she asked innocently.

"It was apparently during a time that he and my mother were going through a rough patch," Bella suggested. "Lynda threw herself at him, and my father, being vulnerable at he was, took the bait." Bella's eyes narrowed. "She threatened to reveal their dirty little secret to the world—starting with my mother... Panicking over what that might do to her—and everything else my father stood for—he killed Lynda..."

"What?" Stefanie's eyes shot wide at this blunt admission. Had Bella known about this all along?

"I know, I was floored when first learning about it," Bella told her, a catch to her tone of voice. "More tea?" she asked, as if evading the difficult subject matter.

"I'm good," Stefanie said, then picked up the cup to sip a bit more of it for effect. "Go on…" she urged her.

"Okay." Bella nodded. "Anyway, my dad made the confession in a journal that he kept. I'd known about the journal for years, but never gave much thought as to what was in it. Not till after he passed away. He confessed to poisoning Lynda with the thallium sulfate that Sidney Sedwick hooked him up with—then made an effort to blame her death on Wendell Braison, knowing that Lynda was a follower of the Braison Family at the time and their controversial lifestyle."

"Wow," was all Stefanie could say at the moment. "So, you found the journal?"

"If only that were true." Bella's face contorted. "Then everything might have turned out differently." She sighed, meditative. "As it is, this all only came to light when I discovered that Mia O'Dell, my father's former housekeeper, had stolen the journal. She intended to blackmail me for a considerable amount to get the journal back. Or else, she planned to hand it over to the police as a two decades old confession to murder. Neither were particularly good choices for me to chew on and swallow—or spit out…"

Stefanie batted her lashes. "So what did you do, Bella?"

"The only thing I could do," she answered boldly, flashing her eyes at Stefanie. "I killed her!" She sighed. "Or participated in killing her with some able-bodied help—"

"What?" Stefanie tried to digest what she had just heard while absentmindedly taking another sip of the tea. Who helped her? "Please tell me you didn't go that far?"

"I had no choice," Bella insisted. "Okay, my dad was a

bastard. But he was *still* my father. I wasn't about to allow a money grabber to put the squeeze on me—or else!"

"There's always a choice." Stefanie's mouth hung open with disbelief. "How could you?"

"It wasn't that difficult, truly." Bella's voice grew dark. "I had my family's legacy to think about. And since most people bought into the notion that Lynda Boxleitner's death was directly attributable to her involvement with the Braison Family, I wanted to keep it that way. As Mia also happened to be a member of the cult, it made sense to connect her death to them as well—make it appear that both women were poisoned by someone within the cult—albeit twenty years apart. Fentanyl was much easier to come by these days, especially if you knew where to get it."

Stefanie batted her lashes. "Did you know where to get fentanyl?"

"Not exactly." Bella wrinkled her nose. "Fortunately, the person I aligned myself with did."

"Who?" She locked eyes with her, while pondering who would help her kill someone. "Is it Kenneth Braison?" Stefanie found that hard to fathom, considering everything else she had just heard. But Bella seemed to have no trouble getting what—or whom—she wanted, so anything was possible.

"Actually, it's Juan Barrientos," Bella told her proudly.

"Juan?" Stefanie looked at her with shock. "And you?"

Bella laughed. "It's not what you think. Not really. Yes, we hooked up a couple of times and that's it. This was all it took to have him wrapped around my little finger," she said satisfyingly, lifting up her pinkie to make her point. "It's primarily a business arrangement. He's helped me take care of some problems…and he's got his own agenda. So there you have it."

Stefanie was beginning to feel a little queasy, but thought it must have been an unsettled stomach with what she'd just been told. She peered at Bella and asked point-blank, "So you and Juan poisoned Jasmine, too?"

Bella sighed. "She asked way too many questions and became a liability. Beyond that, Jasmine's death was another way to point the finger at the Braison Family as being responsible for poisonous deaths across two generations—"

"This is crazy," Stefanie said, unable to keep the thought to herself. "You'll never get away with it…"

"Don't be too sure about that," Bella boasted confidently. "Everything's going according to plan—"

What's that supposed to mean? Stefanie wondered. How could Bella truly believe she would be able to keep her deadly secrets? "If you're expecting me to keep this to myself—I can't do that. Campbell needs to know what you and Juan have been doing…"

Bella chuckled. "I'm afraid he won't find out from you, Stefanie… You see, unfortunately, you've become a liability, too. If only you hadn't fortuitously come upon Mia on Founder's Day, you and I could have maintained a wonderful and lasting friendship. But you did find her—and in the process, came into Campbell's orbit—putting a real damper on our camaraderie. I knew it was only a matter of time before it would come to an end. That time is now…"

As if on cue, Stefanie found herself feeling even sicker, shaky and starting to perspire. She leveled her eyes at Bella and demanded, "What have you done to me?" The answer came to her before a response came from her unexpected new adversary.

Fluttering her lashes, Bella answered cruelly, "I took the liberty of spicing your herbal tea with enough fentanyl laced with carfentanil powder—and even some fentanyl liquid put in for good measure—so you'd die from an overdose. Like Mia and Jasmine—as well as Lynda from back in the day—you'll show up naked in Reston Hills Park as another victim of the Braison Family..."

Stefanie tried to get to her feet, intent upon leaving the house, but fell back onto the sectional as dizziness overcame her. She tried to remove the cell phone from her jeans, but Bella beat her to the punch, grabbing it first.

"Sorry, can't let you warn Campbell," she hissed. "It would ruin everything..."

Just then, Stefanie heard a door slam shut and footsteps coming their way. Moments later, she watched as Juan Barrientos entered the den.

Bella narrowed her eyes at him. "What took you so long?"

"Had to be creative in getting out of the compound without too many questions being asked," he explained. "Sorry."

Bella's nostrils flared. "Anyway, you're here now."

Juan regarded Stefanie and asked, "She give you any problems?"

"None that I couldn't handle," Bella responded succinctly.

Stefanie, who found herself even struggling to speak, forced out words anyhow. "Ca-Campbell is ne-never going to buy that I OD'd on fentanyl—no matter h-how you try to frame it," she stammered.

Bella laughed and bragged, "I can be very persuasive when I want to be with Juan's help. He'll plant some of your clothing—even your cell phone—and fentanyl powder and liquid at Kenneth Braison's ranch house…and I'll insist that it be thoroughly searched. When the evidence is found, Kenneth will be arrested for your murder and, undoubtedly, Mia's and Jasmine's, too. I'll get what I want in protecting my family's legacy and Juan will assume the leadership role in the Braison Family. It's a win-win. But not for you, Stefanie, I'm sorry to say."

"I don't think you are!" Stefanie spat out, furrowing her brow while peering at Bella. "Neither of you!"

She glared at Juan, who grinned at her maliciously and said, "You're right—not sorry at all. It is what it is." He gazed at Bella. "Let's get this over with."

"Okay," she uttered unfeelingly.

Stefanie, her heart racing wildly, life flashing before her eyes, tried getting to her feet again as the effects of the poison given to her spread like cancer throughout her entire body. But before she could even contemplate her next move, in what seemed to be a truly hopeless situation—one in which Campbell was likely none the wiser and, as such, unable to come to her aid in time—Stefanie passed out.

CAMPBELL STILL FELT UNSETTLED, even after they got Judge Ellen Ramiscal to sign a warrant for Juan Barrientos. They had more than enough probable cause to believe that he had purchased the deadly fentanyl mixed with carfentanil—from drug dealer Luther Valdez—that ended up inside of Mia O'Dell and Jasmine Roxburgh, killing them both. Moreover, Mia was seen getting into Barrientos's Volvo XC60 SUV, shortly before her estimated time of death.

The man killed her, intentional or not, Campbell told himself as he headed toward the Braison Family property. That meant that he had to have given Jasmine the lethal drug combo, too. So was this the work of a serial killer who was intentionally getting rid of cult members who had become expendable? Or did Barrientos have another purpose in mind for the OD poisonings made to resemble the fatal poisoning of Lynda Boxleitner?

Was he acting alone? Or in concert with another member of the Braison Family, if not Kenneth Braison?

Somehow, it didn't figure that Kenneth would direct the execution of two of his likely faithful followers—going against his declaration of a drug-free, peaceful environment—by causing two of them to overdose to death on fentanyl. That would be bad for the business of trying to keep current members and recruit new ones, if they stood a good chance of dying by joining the cult. Why jeopardize what Braison might have thought was a good thing going by throwing caution to the wind?

Campbell sat on that thought for a moment, before rejecting the notion that Kenneth was in on this. Much less, condoning it. No, the greater likelihood was that Barrientos was operating outside of Kenneth's knowledge.

Just like his father, Wendell Braison, Campbell had a feeling that Kenneth Braison was getting a raw deal where it concerned the poisoning of Braison Family devotees, other controversies of the cult notwithstanding.

But what am I missing? Campbell asked himself as he pulled onto South Petriss Road, nearing the Braison Family ranch. Something told him that there was an element or two that had yet to be fully fleshed out in hitting the mark in the investigation.

Unless they could pinpoint this soon, other followers of the Family could still be in danger. Or someone from the outside, such as Stefanie—who had taken an interest in the cult for altruistic reasons after being indirectly connected to the deaths of two members. Campbell felt comfort knowing that she was at least in a safe space at the moment, spending time with Bella.

He drove up to the gate, alongside another detective's vehicle, while ready to track down Juan Barrientos and bring him in for questioning.

Chapter Eighteen

Campbell and Detective Xander Wilde, a forty-three-year-old African American who was tall and muscular with a shaved head, entered the Braison Family compound. Apart from their Glock 19 pistols, they were armed with an arrest warrant for Juan Barrientos. Backup officers were on standby.

"Think there will be any resistance?" Xander asked, his brown eyes gazing at the property, its members seemingly going about their business nonchalantly.

"Shouldn't be, if they know what's good for them." Though he didn't dismiss the notion altogether, Campbell didn't believe that Kenneth Braison was looking for a fight. Especially when it appeared that Barrientos's wrongdoing was more of a solo effort than representing the Family, per se. "Let's find Barrientos."

With no luck and no cooperation, they wound up running into Kenneth outside his ranch house. He was in the company of a tall, slender and attractive twentysomething female with long raven hair in a U-shaped cut and big hazel eyes.

Kenneth peered disapprovingly at Campbell. "Detective Sawyer…"

Without beating around the bush, Campbell said

tersely, "This is Detective Wilde. We have a warrant for Juan Barrientos's arrest. Where is he?"

"He's not here." Kenneth narrowed his eyes. "What's this all about?"

Xander responded with an edge to his tone. "We believe that Barrientos bought the fentanyl in powdered and liquid form, that Mia O'Dell and Jasmine Roxburgh OD'd on, from a known drug dealer."

"What?" Kenneth's jaw dropped. "There must be some mistake—"

"It's no mistake!" Campbell's forehead creased. "Apart from Barrientos being identified by the drug dealer, we also have him on surveillance video picking up Mia not far from Kieke's Nightclub shortly before she ended up dead from the lethal fentanyl concoction."

Kenneth set his jaw. "How could Juan betray my trust like this?" he asked in disbelief. "And do such harm to members of the Braison Family? Why...?"

"You'll have to ask him that," Campbell said, sensing that the cult leader wasn't the wiser to what his likely ambitious right-hand man was up to. "Now, where can we find Barrientos?"

"He's out doing some personal business. I never asked what that was..."

"Maybe you should have," Xander spoke harshly. "Could be that he's buying more drugs to poison your followers."

Kenneth bristled at the suggestion. "You're right," he muttered. "I thought Juan had my back—our backs... Looks like I totally misjudged his intentions as a disloyal member of the Family..."

"Apparently so." Campbell wondered how the cult

leader could have missed the mark there. He favored him musingly. This seemed as good a time as any to come clean with him on another matter. "Speaking of misjudging—regarding the cold case homicide of Lynda Boxleitner, your father, Wendell Braison, is no longer considered a person of interest."

Kenneth's brow shot up. "Since when?"

"Since new info surfaced and the case and culprit pointed in an entirely different direction," Campbell said sincerely. He wished Braison's son hadn't been forced to carry the burden of his father's possible guilt through the years, but he now had the opportunity to move past it. While facing new demons, what with the current investigation tying a member of the Braison Family to two poisonous deaths.

"I see," Kenneth said, then added bitterly, "Better late than never."

"Yeah." Campbell glanced at Xander, then looked at the young woman beside Kenneth, who eyed him back.

She uttered tentatively with a British accent, "My name's Siobhan Froggatt. There's something I need to say—"

"I'm listening," Campbell told her, watching Kenneth's uneasy—and perhaps possessive—reaction before turning back to her face.

Siobhan tucked some loose strands of hair behind an ear and said, "If what you say about Juan giving Jasmine and Mia deadly drugs is true, it makes me concerned about Lois Ohashi, the Family member he shares a cabin with…" She took a breath, venturing a glance at Kenneth. "Lois told me in confidence that she took a look at Juan's cell phone while he was sleeping and discovered through text messages that he was seeing someone on the outside… Maybe Juan will try to poison Lois so he can be with the other woman—"

Campbell didn't discount her fears about what Barrientos was capable of. Fixing his eyes on Siobhan, he asked thoughtfully, "Did Lois happen to get the name of this woman Barrientos is involved with?"

Siobhan regarded Kenneth, as if for permission to answer and he nodded with approval and maybe curiosity, before she responded confidently, "Bella Reston."

Bella and Barrientos? Campbell thought with shock after having already returned to his SUV, where he was riding solo. He never saw that coming. Apparently, neither did Kenneth Braison, based upon his negative reaction. How did those two come to be romantically involved, when Campbell thought that she and golfer Russell Kercheval were an item? And just what else were Bella and Juan up to? Or had been?

More disturbing to Campbell at the moment was that Stefanie had texted him earlier to say that she was going to pay Bella a visit. Now he was having trouble reaching Stefanie by phone. Was there a legitimate reason for this? Would Bella—and her latest lover—actually try to harm Stefanie?

While the search was underway for Juan Barrientos and his blue Volvo XC60 SUV, with a BOLO alert out for him and his vehicle, Campbell was about to head over to Bella's house, when his cell phone rang. He took it out of his blazer and saw that it was Georgina.

Her voice was anxious as she said, "We just got a bead on Barrientos's SUV. An automated license plate reader picked up his vehicle on Hepmore Avenue, headed toward Reston Hills Park. There appears to be at least two people inside the vehicle—"

That news caused Campbell's heart to skip a beat. He drew a deep breath and said, "Turns out that Juan Barrientos is involved in a romantic relationship with Bella Reston."

"Seriously?" Georgina voiced in surprise.

"Yeah, his Braison Family girlfriend read his texts and discovered it."

"Do you think Bella is a party to the deadly drug overdoses?" Georgina asked. "Or could she too become a victim of Barrientos?"

Campbell considered the two possibilities. Having known Bella, she didn't at all strike him as the victim type. At least not where it concerned drug abuse. Or being conned by Juan Barrientos. It seemed more likely that she would be calling the shots in their relationship. That included wanting Mia and Jasmine dead for some bizarre reason that had to be about Bella's father, Stuart Reston, his former lover, Lynda Boxleitner, and the opportunistic entanglements involving the Braison Family.

After a long moment, Campbell replied with conviction, "I think that Bella and Barrientos are in this together. Right down to obtaining the fentanyl mixed with carfentanil—and poisoning Mia and Jasmine. I also fear that they may have abducted Stefanie, drugged her, and are taking her to the park to leave her for dead like the others." He sighed. "I need all available units—along with a SWAT team, crisis negotiator and EMS—to get to Reston Hills Park immediately, which is where I'm headed right now…"

"You've got it," Georgina said tensely.

"On the chance that Stefanie is being kept at Bella's house or was able to return home, get the same personnel to both places—just in case..."

"Okay. I'm close to Bella's house, so I'll pop over there myself and take a look, while waiting for backup."

"All right."

Campbell disconnected. He pressed down on the accelerator, knowing that every second could be a matter of life and death. He didn't even want to think about his world without Stefanie being in it for years to come. But how could he not? Hadn't Mia and Jasmine been the victims of fatal fentanyl poisonings in the park? Could Stefanie possibly avoid their fate?

Yes, if at all possible, in any way, shape, or form, he told himself. How else could he get to tell Stefanie how much he loved her? And wanted to build a life with her—and have a family with as many children as she wanted?

Campbell put on even more speed, determined to stop Barrientos from carrying out another death as, undoubtedly, part of Bella's agenda.

STEFANIE FELT WOOZY, sweaty and had trouble breathing as she sat in the back seat of the Volvo, with Juan Barrientos holding her down forcefully and Bella behind the wheel. She was driving them to Reston Hills Park, where they planned to dump her as another fatal overdose victim—and blame it entirely on Kenneth Braison and his Family by association.

At some point—probably after she passed out at Bella's house—they removed Stefanie's clothes, so that she was now totally naked and oddly cold in the warm summer-evening temperature. Just like Mia and Jasmine had been forced to endure, humiliation and all.

How long would it take for the authorities—Campbell, especially—to find her body? How would he react to seeing her dead from fentanyl poisoning? Would he accept that Kenneth was responsible for it—ending the life she had hoped to have with Campbell and the children they would produce together—with Bella and Juan getting away with another murder scot-free?

Can I do anything at this point to prevent the inevitable? Stefanie wondered, knowing how weak she felt, while aching all over like living a nightmare. If she could only breathe freely again, before she took her last breath.

Maybe she could find the strength to use her tai chi self-defense skills to fight back.

Or at least die trying to live.

When the SUV drove into the park, Bella found a place to park, then said to Juan in a hardened tone, "Get her out!"

"Okay," he muttered obediently.

Stefanie felt herself being pulled from the car roughly. Then she heard Bella direct him to take her toward the trail—not far from where Stefanie found Mia. Wouldn't it be ironic if they both ran out of life at the same spot, leaving someone else to find Stefanie's corpse.

I can't let that happen...have to do something, her mind told her. As Juan half dragged, half carried her, when Stefanie was on her wobbly legs as he took a quick breather and let down his guard—it was her one and probably only opening to survive her ordeal—so she went for it.

Feeling she was too weak to attempt a joint lock against Juan—knowing that failure would only result in a counter move on his part that would probably be the painful end of her—instead, Stefanie hoped she could hurt him just enough, and maybe Bella, too, to get away from them. Till help arrived.

She used a tai chi technique with her hands to strike him at the bridge of his nose as hard as she could—maybe breaking it—followed in quick succession by a solid blow into his groin. As Juan yelled an expletive, then made an eerie groaning sound, and Bella looked confused, Stefanie took advantage of this to punch her once to the side of the head with enough force to cause Bella to lose her balance and nearly fall, wailing from the discomfort.

As her abductors were sulking, Stefanie tried to make a run for it. She didn't get very far, as her legs were like rubber. And lead weights, all at once.

"Stop her, you idiot!" Bella blared nevertheless, then warned, "But not with the gun! It has to be the fentanyl if we're going to get away with this!"

Stefanie recalled seeing the firearm that he'd pulled briefly from his jacket pocket at Bella's house—meant to intimidate her into cooperating with this diabolical scheme. She tried to move her feet away from them. But they were able to easily close the distance and grab her. Then Juan, angered by the pain she inflicted upon him, slammed a fist into her jaw.

Between that and the effects of the fentanyl poisoning beginning to take full effect, Stefanie fell flat on her face. She went out like a light, while sure she had seen the last of what was once a bright future—one she'd hoped to share with Campbell.

Now none of that seemed possible, now that it appeared

as though Bella and Juan had won the battle—with Stefanie's death being their prize.

CAMPBELL SPOTTED JUAN'S SUV parked haphazardly in the lot. Checking it, he saw no signs of Stefanie. Or, for that matter, Juan Barrientos or Bella Reston. So where were they? And was Stefanie with them—and still alive?

He was left to hope for the best as Campbell locked eyes with Xander Wilde, both detectives converging on the location, holding their firearms and flashlights.

"This place should be swarming with cops shortly," Xander said, as if to make Campbell feel better.

But he didn't. Not till knowing that Stefanie was safe. Wherever she happened to be at the moment.

"Until then," he told Xander, "why don't we split up and see if we come across Barrientos or Bella Reston—"

Xander nodded. "Okay."

Campbell headed into the park in search of Stefanie—who was the best thing to ever happen to him. It certainly felt that way, how she'd managed to warm his heart in ways he never thought possible. Now he only needed to convey that to her. If given the chance.

He heard the sounds of voices up ahead. They were coming his way.

Shining his flashlight in that direction, Campbell saw Bella and Barrientos. But not Stefanie.

The two suspects froze when they laid eyes on him.

Pointing the light beam at Barrientos, Campbell said doggedly, "Juan Barrientos, I have a warrant for your arrest on suspicion of causing two drug-induced homicides. Put your hands up—"

Barrientos hesitated. Then abruptly, he pulled a handgun from his jacket and aimed it at him. Before Barrientos ever had a chance to pull the trigger, Campbell shot him once in the chest.

Barrientos went down as the gun flew from his hand. Bella made a move to try to grab it, but Xander, who had shown up at the scene, his own gun pointing at her, spoke in a commanding tone of voice, "I wouldn't try that if I were you—"

Thinking better of ignoring his advice, Bella stayed where she was and Xander quickly came up to her and handcuffed Bella, without resistance.

Campbell, grateful for Xander's teamwork, kept his weapon aimed at Barrientos, who was seriously injured, but still conscious and groaning. The flashlight shone on Barrientos's firearm, which looked to Campbell like a Sig Sauer 10mm pistol. He kicked it farther from Barrientos's reach—for the CSI Unit to take possession of as evidence of the suspect's clear intent to shoot him.

Campbell peered at Barrientos and asked him demandingly, "Where is she—Stefanie Nguyen?"

Barrientos moaned, then responded defiantly, "You tell me."

Campbell took that as an admission that she was in the park. He handcuffed the suspect and stepped toward Bella, who was being held firmly by Xander. "Bella, where's Stefanie?" Campbell demanded.

She glared at him with a snicker and answered coldly, "It's too late for her..."

Campbell wondered how she could go from friend to foe almost in the blink of an eye where it concerned Stefanie. He was sure Bella would put it all out on the table, now that the jig was up.

"Like hell it is," Campbell retorted, not wanting to believe this—against the odds that Stefanie was still alive.

Bella hissed, "Believe it or not, you can't save them all, Campbell—any more than your father could—not even your precious Stefanie…"

Campbell flinched at the venom in Bella's voice, like a cobra. "Stay with them till help arrives," he told Xander. "I'm going to look for Stefanie."

"All right." Xander looked at him. "Find her."

Campbell headed farther into the woods near the river, cutting through the darkness with his flashlight. It occurred to him that he was getting dangerously close to where Mia O'Dell's body was located—by Stefanie. This sent chills down his spine at the thought of the woman he'd fallen in love with suffering the same fate.

When he neared the trail, Campbell spotted the naked figure lying on the ground, motionless. Stefanie. He rushed toward her as his heart sank in seeing her so vulnerable—likely the victim of fentanyl mixed with carfentanil poisoning—and possibly dead.

Campbell put the flashlight in his tactical holster. "Stefanie," he uttered her name in desperation, hoping for a response, while checking for a pulse.

There was one. She was still alive.

Not wanting to waste even one second waiting for paramedics, Campbell removed his blazer to cover Stefanie up as much as possible and then lifted her limp body to carry her back to his SUV or a waiting EMS vehicle.

"I've got you, darling," he uttered mawkishly while getting nothing in return. "Don't you die on me." *I won't let you*, Campbell thought. He prayed that he could keep his word to her and Stefanie would pull through. So that they could get the opportunity to have a wonderful life together, and then some.

Chapter Nineteen

Stefanie was groggy and disoriented, with a sore jaw after being hit, and thirsty, as she opened her eyes—surprised to see that she was still alive. She focused on the attractive oval face of a slender thirtysomething female with a blond balayage A-line haircut and blue eyes behind rectangle glasses standing over her in what Stefanie determined was a hospital bed—and obviously not the morgue.

The woman smiled and said softly. "You're awake…"

"Yes, it appears so," Stefanie quipped, thankfully, noting she was wearing a hospital gown and no longer naked.

"I'm Dr. Hennessy," she told her, wearing a white lab coat. "You were brought into the ER after overdosing on fentanyl."

"I remember all too well." Stefanie made a face, not taking her eyes off the doctor. "So, how did I manage to survive?" She recalled Mia and Jasmine not being so lucky.

"Well, fortunately, paramedics were able to quickly administer naloxone to reverse in time the effects of the fentanyl poisoning or opioid overdose." Dr. Hennessy glanced at a chart and back, smiling. "Aside from some bruising on your face and body and a mild concussion—

all of which should heal—your vital signs are all normal. I'd say you can expect a full recovery."

Stefanie nodded, counting her blessings. "Thank you, Doctor."

"Actually, I'm not the one you should be thanking..." she insisted, and averted her eyes to the other side of the bed.

Stefanie followed suit and gazed at Campbell's handsome face. He grinned at her, but she could see the strain in his features, despite his best efforts to hide it.

"Campbell..." she uttered weakly.

The doctor said coolly, "I'll leave you two alone—"

After she left the room, Campbell moved closer. "Thought I'd lost you for a minute there," he admitted caringly.

Honestly, I thought that, too, Stefanie told herself, against her best wishes. More importantly, she feared she'd lost him forever once the fentanyl and its deadly effects kicked in. She forced a smile. "Afraid you can't get rid of me that easily."

Campbell chuckled. "That's good to know. Especially when I wasn't at all prepared for that to happen anytime soon."

"Neither was I." Stefanie swallowed into her dry throat and coughed. He handed her a cup of water, which, after sitting up, she happily drank. "So, how did you find me...?" *And save my life*, she thought, sensing that Campbell had come to her rescue. In spite of Bella and Juan's plans to the contrary.

He sighed. "We were able to establish that it was Juan Barrientos who—in cahoots with his lover outside of the Braison Family, Bella Reston—gave Mia and Jasmine the deadly combo of fentanyl mixed with carfentanil. A license plate reader spotted Barrientos's SUV headed toward Reston Hills Park. Something told me that he and Bella—whom you were visiting—had planned to kill you as well with a drug overdose…and, I suppose, sail off into the sunset afterward—if you could call getting away with murder that…" Campbell rolled fingers through his hair. "When Barrientos resisted arrest, he was shot. But he'll live. And so will Bella, whether she wants to or not…"

Stefanie was pleased to know that her onetime friend, as well as Juan Barrientos, would face justice for what they had done. "I'm glad they were caught," she said, gazing up at him. "Who knows what else they were capable of."

"Right," he agreed, a contemplative expression crossing his face. "Getting back to how I managed to locate you in the park… With no time to waste, I suppose I just let my instincts guide me…till I came upon you on the trail. You were unconscious, but had a strong enough will for survival that you were able to escape the fate that Bella and Barrientos had in mind—"

Stefanie pondered her brush with death—focusing on Bella's role, in particular, and her dark family legacy. "Bella admitted to conspiring with Juan to kill Mia O'Dell, after Mia tried to blackmail her. This came about when Mia discovered from Stuart Reston's journal—which she stole—that he poisoned to death his lover, Lynda Boxleitner, to prevent Lynda from making public their affair after he refused to leave his wife, Eloise Reston, for her. Mia, who was struggling to make ends meet, in spite of her involvement with the Braison Family, hoped to cash in on her knowledge."

Campbell frowned and said matter-of-factly, "But Bella, wanting to protect her family heritage, rejected this—choosing to kill Mia instead..."

Stefanie nodded. "Bella wasn't about to allow Mia to ruin everything her family stood for. Using the Braison Family angle, Bella tried to tie Mia's fatal poisoning to the poisoning death of Lynda Boxleitner—to make it seem that both were orchestrated by the father-son cult leaders, Wendell and Kenneth Braison. Jasmine was poisoned with fentanyl after she asked too many questions and Bella panicked that the truth might come out. Also, it didn't hurt if another drug-induced death could be connected to the Braison Family to further try and influence the investigation."

Campbell took a breath, meeting her eyes. "Why did Bella want you dead, too?" Before Stefanie could answer, he said intuitively, "Let me guess... Bella felt further threatened by your interest in the investigation and how that might come back on her?"

"Yes, something like that," she told him. "Apparently, Bella became paranoid by my talking to Jasmine and any type of rippling effect that might expose her. Then there was also her determination to make the Braison Family wrongfully culpable for past and present sins in the poisonings. She hoped to use my death to set up Kenneth Braison—short of tattooing his initials on my arm—by planting evidence at his house and making sure it was found. All to protect her family's good name. Though just how good it is, is questionable."

"Yeah, quite." Campbell rolled his eyes. "And what would Barrientos get for his trouble?"

"Control of the Braison Family and all that comes with being the cult's leader," Stefanie told him.

"I thought as much, when trying to piece it all together." Campbell ran hand across his jawline. "But they failed to achieve their goals, with both now in custody and facing years behind bars."

"Good." Stefanie adjusted herself in the bed and looked up at him, while thinking about them and their own future prospects. "So, when will I be released?"

"As far as I'm aware, the process is already in the works for you to be discharged," Campbell answered equably. He sat on the side of the bed, and held one of her hands affectionately. "But before they let you out of here, there's something I've been dying to say to you…"

"Oh?" She met his gaze, interest piqued. "What might that be?"

"Just that I've fallen in love with you, Stefanie Nguyen," he expressed soulfully.

Stefanie beamed. "Is that so?"

"Yeah, definitely so." He kissed her hand. "When I feared that I might never have gotten the opportunity to say that—had Bella and Barrientos gotten their way—I promised myself that I wouldn't allow myself to miss the chance again as soon as it presented itself to express my true feelings in living color. And any other way to say I love you, Stefanie."

She blushed, squeezing his fingers. "Well, I'm in love with you, too, Campbell," she cadenced.

He grinned crookedly. "Really?"

"Yes, really." Stefanie was filled with happiness. "I also feared that I might have lost that window to tell you how I felt," she said tearfully "But now that the window has reopened, I won't wait for it to nearly shut again before putting my heart on the line, forever and a day." She drew a breath and fixed his eyes. "I do love you and always will—whatever our destiny is…"

Campbell's face lit up with raw emotion. "In that case, we can't go wrong, as I'm with you all the way!"

He leaned over and gave her a hard kiss on the mouth that Stefanie embraced for all the strength she could muster. In time, she hoped to be able to show him just how much she cared for him through long, tender kisses and otherwise. But for now, this was more than enough for her to hang onto and relish to her heart's content, while knowing that Campbell felt the same way, through and through.

THE NEXT MORNING, in Harriette's Café, Campbell sat with Gloria at a table, going over the case and its unexpected twists and turns. He knew she had more than a passing interest, given her time with the department, dating back to the murder of Lynda Boxleitner. And how that managed to work its way to the present drug-related homicides.

While nibbling on a Danish pastry, Gloria batted her lashes and said, as if still trying to come to terms with it, "Bella Reston and Juan Barrientos…who would have thunk it?"

"True." Campbell bit into a cinnamon roll, then took a sip of his coffee. "I guess power and privilege—not necessarily in that order—makes for strange bedfellows."

"I suppose." She tasted her green tea. "The important thing is that you figured out many of the sordid details and stopped them from adding another victim to the madness."

"Yeah." He took a breath. The thought that he had

come so close to losing Stefanie made Campbell almost nauseous. Being deprived of expressing his love and receiving the same in return was almost too much to bear. But they had come out on the other end, stronger than ever. In spite of Bella's and Barrientos's efforts to the contrary. "Now we just need to put them away for good. Or at least for the better part of the life they have left."

"That would be nice," Gloria agreed before taking another bite of the Danish. "But you can be sure that Bella Reston—at least—will have the best lawyers that money can buy to try and worm her way out of this."

"I expect as much," Campbell acknowledged. "But money can only go so far."

"You're right. But in this instance, as far as her admission to Stefanie that Mia O'Dell was killed because of blackmail regarding Stuart Reston's confession in a journal to murdering Lynda Boxleitner—it's Stefanie's word against Bella's, who would surely deny having ever said such. It would never hold up in court on that basis alone." Gloria sipped her tea and sat back. "I'm guessing that the journal in question was found by Bella or Barrientos and destroyed."

"That's always a possibility," Campbell allowed musingly. "But since Bella is strongly invested in the Reston family history, I suspect that she would have wanted to hold on to her father's journal—even if damaging to him and the Reston legacy—to preserve it from one generation to the next. Especially if Bella, so full of herself, believed that she would succeed in keeping the onus for Boxleitner's murder entirely on Wendell Braison—by adding some new homicides to the mix to further protect the family's place in this town—and it would never come back to haunt her. Meaning that she likely still has Reston's journal in her possession."

Gloria nodded. "You make a good point." She ate another piece of Danish. "I hope you can find it and use it as evidence to help make the case."

"Me too." Campbell liked his chances. But there was more to it than that. "Beyond finally giving Lynda Boxleitner the peace in death that she deserves after all these years, Bella has more serious concerns for her attorneys to deal with. She's on the hook—along with Juan Barrientos—for the lethal fentanyl poisonings of Mia O'Dell and Jasmine Roxburgh. And the attempted murder of Stefanie Nguyen. No amount of dirty family money will be enough to worm her way out of that hole."

"I agree," Gloria said, tilting her face. "Bella Reston will get what she deserves, as will Juan Barrientos. Maybe then, this town—and even the Braison Family—can get back to some semblance of normalcy and move forward."

"That's the hope," Campbell said, sipping his coffee contemplatively. He particularly liked the part about moving forward—which is exactly what he hoped to do with Stefanie, now that they had gotten past life and death issues that, for a moment or two, had left things between them hanging in the balance.

IN SEPTEMBER, STEFANIE went with Campbell to visit his father and ride horses. It was just her second time ever getting on a horse. The first was a month earlier when they visited the ranch and she and Campbell went on a trail ride on Appaloosas. Though a bit sore, she truly loved the experience, as the horse was gentle and it gave her an opportunity to spread her wings in further bonding—not only with Campbell, but with Mason and his lovely partner, Sally. They made her feel welcome, as though part of the family.

Stefanie relished this, eager to have the same type of strong connection she once had with her own mother and father, whom she missed more than she could say, though feeling they were always angels on her shoulders. Just as Edward was, in wanting her to be happy in life. Which she was, knowing how precious each day could be, when it so easily could be taken away.

Campbell was just as thrilled that she had warmed to his father—and she was delighted to see that the two men had put aside any differences they may have had through the years and were forging stronger ties themselves.

In Stefanie's mind, knowing that a cold case and current case between father and son had merged into one and been closed, more or less, made their relationship that much stronger.

It seemed as if Bella, on the advice of expensive lawyers, had cut a deal in confessing to her part in the deaths of Mia O'Dell and Jasmine Roxburgh. *And the intent to kill me with the same fentanyl poisoning*, Stefanie thought as her horse trotted across the meadow. As a result, instead of spending the rest of her life behind bars, Bella would still have the opportunity to one day go free. But would still pay a very high price for the bad decisions she made. Her family legacy—thanks in part to Stuart Reston's journal and the testimony of his former gardener, Sidney Sedwick—was now in tatters and likely never to be fully repaired as the town's namesake.

Juan Barrientos didn't get off nearly as easily. With his case transferred to federal jurisdiction and a solid case against him for serious drug-related offenses, including two drug-induced homicides—and the willingness of drug trafficker Luther Valdez to testify against him—Juan confessed. Even with that, he would not see the light of day again with a sentence of life imprisonment.

Stefanie found solace in that, knowing Juan had tried to kill her and would never get that opportunity again. In spite of him having been used by Bella to achieve her own objectives—with frequent phone calls and spicy text messages to Juan that were produced as evidence to illustrate the romantic nature of their relationship—it was Juan who acquired the deadly fentanyl and carfentanil from Valdez that nearly sent Stefanie to an early grave. *How can I not hold him responsible to a slightly higher degree?* she asked herself, as a part of her wanted to believe that in an alternate reality, she and Bella could have truly ended up as real friends.

"Are you all right?" Campbell asked in earnest, riding alongside her.

Stefanie gazed at him, looking every bit the cowboy with his cowboy hat on and clothing to match. She flashed a genuine, loving smile and answered, "Better than ever! Race you back?"

He laughed. "You're on."

She chuckled as her horse trotted off ahead of him, pretty sure he would catch her. As surely as he had captured her heart. And she had captured his.

Epilogue

Founder's Day was gorgeous, in terms of the perfect June temperature and not a cloud in the baby blue sky to be spotted. The annual celebration didn't miss a beat as the locals and visitors alike gathered in Reston Hills Park, following a big parade down Hepmore Avenue, where floats, dignitaries, marching bands, riders, walkers, students and onlookers came together to make it the best parade ever in town.

Stefanie and Campbell were joined by Mason and Sally as they moved about by the river, where many of the carnival rides had been set up for children and adults to enjoy, while viewing the boats out in the water that were taking advantage of ideal conditions.

"I can't believe it's been a year since I found Mia's body," Stefanie said, sharing a bag of walnuts and pistachios with Campbell. She hated to be on a momentary down note, but was sure that the anniversary of the tragedy—as well as one from twenty-one years earlier—did not go unnoticed by him. Or Mason, for that matter.

"Yeah, I know," Campbell muttered, a slice of remorse in his voice. "It was definitely a day to forget for most of us in town as if anyone ever could," he said truthfully.

Mason looked at him and said earnestly, "We all had to endure a rough patch, son—spanning more than two decades—but we've dealt with it and come out stronger, each and every one of us."

Campbell nodded. "True. It's brought us closer together, Dad, and for that, I'm forever grateful."

Mason grinned, tapping his shoulder. "I feel the same."

"Me too." Sally smiled, holding Mason's hand. "Absolutely, I know that we're stronger because of it," she told him, "and I wouldn't want it any other way."

"Neither would I," he voiced affectionately.

Campbell turned to Stefanie and said candidly, "For me, even with all that went down—including seeing Bella and Juan held accountable for their crimes—the silver lining was meeting you, Stefanie. One thing might never have happened without the other. Can't imagine you not being in my life now."

"Me neither." She blushed, pushing past the misfortune that befell Mia O'Dell and Jasmine Roxburgh, in favor of a perhaps once-in-a-lifetime opportunity to get to know him on a deep level that grew deeper over time. "The good thing is, you don't have to imagine that. I'm not going anywhere."

"Actually, there is somewhere I'd like you to go—with me," Campbell said, gazing down at her intently.

"Oh?" She met his blue eyes curiously. "Where would you like to go?" Perhaps back to his place for some afternoon delight? Or hers for the same?

"The Ferris wheel," he told her bluntly.

She raised a brow in surprise. "The Ferris wheel?"

"Yeah. Haven't been on one of those since I was a kid." Campbell flashed her a grin askew. "Guess you bring out the kid in me. So what do you say?"

"Go on," Mason prodded her lightheartedly. "Live dangerously—just a little."

Sally chuckled. "I say go for it, Stefanie. We'll go, too, if it makes you feel more comfortable."

Stefanie laughed. "That won't be necessary." She knew she would be more than comfortable being on the Ferris wheel with Campbell by her side. "Let's do it," she told him enthusiastically.

"Okay." He grinned, taking her hand. "Come with me."

CAMPBELL WAS ON pins and needles as he led Stefanie onto the Ferris wheel. Sitting next to her, he went through the usual chitchat as the carnival ride began to go up, stopping slowly but surely, for everyone to experience life at the top. It offered a great view of the Founder's Day festivities and the activities taking place on the Beeks River.

He thought briefly about the last year that seemed to whiz by in some ways. Not so much others. It had seen a cold case and present time case merge together just enough to put both to rest and imprison the perpetrators that were still alive. A disgraced Stuart Reston escaped justice. But he had managed to taint the Reston name, as had Bella—which would never be the same again. Fortunately, Arthur Reston—the town's founder—was not being held accountable for the sins of his descendants. Meaning Reston Hills would live on for future generations who only wanted to make a good life for themselves like those in other small towns across the country.

Campbell turned his thoughts to the gorgeous woman beside him and how she had managed to overcome her brush with death as a survivor, who showed him the love he'd never experience before and wanted to hang onto for the rest of his life.

With that in mind, knowing how strongly he felt for her, Campbell waited for the Ferris wheel to come to a stop at the very top. He turned to Stefanie and said tenderly, "I love you, Stefanie Nguyen, which I've probably told you more times than you care to hear for nearly a year now... But the only way I can do the actions-speak-louder-than words thing is to give you this—" He pulled a small box out of his plaid sport coat and opened it to reveal an oval-cut diamond engagement ring in 14k yellow gold. Having already given his father a heads-up on his intentions, Campbell hoped she was ready to give marriage a second chance at happiness. He asked her smoothly, "Will you marry me, Stefanie—and make the happiest man in the world—which has far greater reach than Reston Hills alone?"

"Yes, and a thousand more yesses!" Stefanie cried out joyously and kissed him solidly on the mouth. "I will marry you, Campbell Sawyer—which will make me by far the happiest woman in the world today, Reston Hills notwithstanding!"

"Marvelous!" His voice rose a couple of octaves with emotion. "Music to my ears."

She eagerly held out her ring finger for him to place the engagement ring on, and he did so, for a perfect fit.

"I love it," Stefanie said exuberantly. "Almost as much as I love you, my darling!"

"That deep love works both ways," Campbell told her affectionately. "And so much more!"

"Always nice to hear those words," she expressed.

"Then I'll keep them coming and coming," he promised, cupped her cheeks and kissed Stefanie passionately, hardly aware that the Ferris wheel had started to move again.

* * * * *

Get up to 4 Free Books!

We'll send you 2 free books from each series you try PLUS a free Mystery Gift.

FREE Value Over **$25**

Both the **Harlequin Intrigue**® and **Harlequin**® **Romantic Suspense** series feature compelling novels filled with heart-racing action-packed romance that will keep you on the edge of your seat.

YES! Please send me 2 FREE novels from the Harlequin Intrigue or Harlequin Romantic Suspense series and my FREE gift (gift is worth about $10 retail). After receiving them, if I don't wish to receive any more books, I can return the shipping statement marked "cancel." If I don't cancel, I will receive 6 brand-new Harlequin Intrigue Larger-Print books every month and be billed just $7.19 each in the U.S. or $7.99 each in Canada, or 4 brand-new Harlequin Romantic Suspense books every month and be billed just $6.39 each in the U.S. or $7.19 each in Canada, a savings of 20% off the cover price. It's quite a bargain! Shipping and handling is just 50¢ per book in the U.S. and $1.25 per book in Canada.* I understand that accepting the 2 free books and gift places me under no obligation to buy anything. I can always return a shipment and cancel at any time by calling the number below. The free books and gift are mine to keep no matter what I decide.

Choose one:
- ☐ **Harlequin Intrigue Larger-Print** (199/399 BPA G36Y)
- ☐ **Harlequin Romantic Suspense** (240/340 BPA G36Y)
- ☐ **Or Try Both!** (199/399 & 240/340 BPA G36Z)

Name (please print)

Address   Apt. #

City   State/Province   Zip/Postal Code

Email: Please check this box ☐ if you would like to receive newsletters and promotional emails from Harlequin Enterprises ULC and its affiliates. You can unsubscribe anytime.

Mail to the Harlequin Reader Service:
IN U.S.A.: P.O. Box 1341, Buffalo, NY 14240-8531
IN CANADA: P.O. Box 603, Fort Erie, Ontario L2A 5X3

Want to explore our other series or interested in ebooks? Visit www.ReaderService.com or call 1-800-873-8635.

---

*Terms and prices subject to change without notice. Prices do not include sales taxes, which will be charged (if applicable) based on your state or country of residence. Canadian residents will be charged applicable taxes. Offer not valid in Quebec. This offer is limited to one order per household. Books received may not be as shown. Not valid for current subscribers to the Harlequin Intrigue or Harlequin Romantic Suspense series. All orders subject to approval. Credit or debit balances in a customer's account(s) may be offset by any other outstanding balance owed by or to the customer. Please allow 4 to 6 weeks for delivery. Offer available while quantities last.

Your Privacy—Your information is being collected by Harlequin Enterprises ULC, operating as Harlequin Reader Service. For a complete summary of the information we collect, how we use this information and to whom it is disclosed, please visit our privacy notice located at https://corporate.harlequin.com/privacy-notice. Notice to California Residents – Under California law, you have specific rights to control and access your data. For more information on these rights and how to exercise them, visit https://corporate.harlequin.com/california-privacy. For additional information for residents of other U.S. states that provide their residents with certain rights with respect to personal data, visit https://corporate.harlequin.com/other-state-residents-privacy-rights/.